JUST SAY YES

Also by Judith McDaniel

Metamorphosis, Reflections on Recovery
Sanctuary, A Journey
The Stories We Hold Secret (coeditor)
Winter Passage
November Woman

JUST SAY YES

A NOVEL

JUDITH McDANIEL

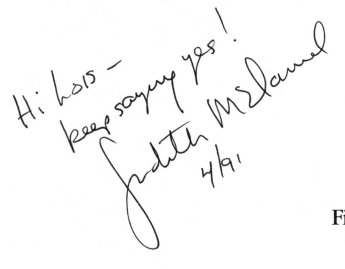

Hi Lois —
keep saying yes!
Judith McDaniel
4/91

**Firebrand
Books**
Ithaca, New York

Book and cover design by Betsy Bayley
Typesetting by Bets Ltd.

Printed in the United States on acid-free paper by McNaughton & Gunn

Acknowledgments

I would like to thank the many women who helped and support-
ed me while I was writing this novel. Some have not been named,
but each will recognize, I believe, her own contribution.

Thank you—
    for reading the earliest draft and encouraging me to keep at it—
Bernice Mennis, Rachel Guido deVries, Barbara Smith;
    for reading later drafts and helping with the details—Judith Mazza,
Maureen O'Brien, Elly Bulkin, Claudia Brenner, Paula Sawyer, Phyl-
lis Rusnock, Nancy Pringle, Noreen Ruff;
    for suggesting the title—Claudia Brenner, Anne Rhodes;
    and finally to the girls at the beach for providing the inspiration—
Marie, Sandy, Celia, Joanne, Gloria, Meredith, Sue, Mary, Judith,
Maureen, Nancy, Janis, Michael (who loaned us his binoculars), and
others too numerous to mention. You were all quite wonderful that summer.

While a community of women contributed to this novel, I alone
am responsible for its direction and execution, including any out-
rages, errors, or mistatements.

                                                      Judith McDaniel
                                                      December 1990

Chapter One

"**S**he showed you WHAT?"

"Angie, keep it down." Lindsey looked over her bare shoulder at the couple on the lavender blanket twenty feet away. Good. One of them had headphones on and the other seemed to be sound asleep. Lindsey sifted some sand through her fingers and scootched her belly around on the blanket to make a little depression for her hip bones. Shit. She knew she shouldn't have said anything to Angie. It was all too embarrassing.

"I'm sorry." Angie sounded contrite. "Just think of me as an interested researcher, Lin. I mean, I am an interested researcher. I wish someone had done something like that for me when I was just starting to make love to women. I mean, we aren't born knowing how, no matter what the propaganda is, you know? They say, well, she's a woman just like you are and so you know what would please her, right? But goddess knows," Angie heaved a sigh of profound despair and turned over on her towel, lifting her well-tanned breasts to the sunlight, "I mean, women are so *various.*" She stressed the word by making her voice deep and husky. "Which is wonderful, you know, but you could spend a lifetime figuring it all out, so it was great of her to show you, you know what I mean?"

Lindsey nodded thoughtfully, wondering how much of Angie's effusion she could trust.

"Well, was it in any place unusual? Just tell me that." Angie looked anxious, and Lindsey decided it would be better not to leave her with the wrong impression.

7

"No, Angie, for god's sake. She said her clitoris was a little higher than normal. That's all." Lindsey tried for a clinical and detached tone of voice. "When a woman's clitoris is high like that, usually it's more covered by the hood, and so if she likes direct stimulation, her partner has to pull the hood way up. That's all." She hoped she sounded bored and indifferent, which certainly had *not* described her last night when it was all happening.

"Oh, right." Angie waved her hand as though she'd known that all her life. "Your back looks a little red. You better turn over."

Lindsey grunted but didn't move. She wasn't sure whether there was more to this conversation, and she didn't want to talk about sex if her body was exposed. But Angie seemed to be drifting off into her own thoughts. Probably it was safe. Lindsey turned her breasts up to the warm sun and let the gentle offshore breeze caress them. She still didn't know how she felt about last night. Should she be embarrassed? Pleased? Angry? Was she in love? No, she could answer that right away. Would she see her again tonight? That was a more reasonable question, and Lindsey didn't know the answer. She set her wristwatch alarm for twenty-five minutes and let herself doze into the memory of the night before.

Ra's blonde straight hair floated across her forehead and was cut back to reveal her small ears, one with a perfectly gorgeous turquoise crescent moon riding on the lobe. Lindsey brought the order of steamers to their table and joked with the three women about the best way to tease the meaty clam morsels out of their shells. "Fingers," she had insisted with a shy grin and a lifted eyebrow. "I don't think you need an . . ." She paused and put the wine glass in front of the blonde, carefully looking down the neckline of her open silk shirt as she spoke, ". . . an implement." They had all chuckled appreciatively. You're learning, girl, Lindsey congratulated herself. They're going to leave a nice tip, you bet. And they had. The blonde stayed behind, fussing with the check, and when Lindsey came back to the table, she took Lindsey's hand, laid the bills and check in her open palm, then closed her fingers around Lindsey's fist. "My name's Ra, Lindsey. What time do you get finished here?"

Lindsey could feel the flush rising from her nipples right up her neck to her cheeks. Thank god she had some tan. "Around eleven."

"Good. Can I pick you up then for a couple of dances at Miz-moon's?" Ra's gaze was steady and friendly and casual.

Oh, god. Here it was, just like Sheila had warned her, and she hadn't even been in P-town two weeks yet. "Sure. That would be great, Ra." Oh my god, who said that? Was it her? What had she done? And then it was too late. Ra was still smiling, but she had waved and was moving across the restaurant, leaving Lindsey to pry the check money out of her sweaty palm.

Lindsey sighed deeply and shifted her arms in the sand. The rest of the evening had been a pleasant blur. Other customers. Closing up. The bar. The walk with Ra in the moonlight across town to her guesthouse, their fingers linked casually, hips bumping into one another as they walked. The single candle Ra lit with a flourish before she turned toward Lindsey. "Hi," she said, as though they'd just met, her smile soft and disarming.

Do something, anything, Lindsey's inner voice prompted her. You're here, aren't you? Don't leave it all to her. And so she had taken Ra's hand and brought it to her lips, nibbled on her fingers, flicked her tongue lightly over the tips. "Mmmm," she murmured, "lobster."

Ra had laughed a little, and then—what happened? She had taken over. That was what had happened. Lindsey's hands were stopped every time she reached for Ra until Ra had finally whispered, "Let me, O.K.?" And Lindsey had let her. Who could complain? The hands that reached under her T-shirt and pinched her nipples were soft and gentle. She watched as Ra lifted the T-shirt over her breasts, then over her head. Watched the hands move down her bare belly to the belt line of her shorts. Suddenly one hand slid in the front of her shorts and the other was caressing its way down her ass until they met at her now very wet center.

"Nice," Ra whispered, close to her ear. "You're ready for me, aren't you?" Her finger moved slowly, wetly in a circle around the edge of Lindsey's cunt. Lindsey couldn't find her voice in the rising desire flowing up her thighs and focusing right there where Ra's finger was. She moved her head slightly, wanting Ra's lips on her lips, wanting to drown in a long kiss.

"Say it," Ra's voice was teasing. "Say what you want."

"You." Lindsey shuddered with the word.

"More. Tell me what you want me to do to you." The finger was probing a little now, moving in and out, and Lindsey was trapped, standing in this sideways embrace.

Lindsey drew another deep shuddering breath. She didn't think this was the time for conversation. Sheila hadn't warned her about this. Was there an etiquette book for moments like this? A correct dyke vocabulary to explain what she wanted to Ra? One finger began to spread some of the wetness toward her clitoris, moving a short way up the shaft, then back to the wetness, then climbing a little further.

"I want more of that," Lindsey realized. Then, "I want you inside of me. I want your hands and mouth all over my body. I don't want you to stop. Not for a long time."

"Done," Ra agreed with a triumphant smile. And to Lindsey's relief, she slid the interfering shorts down and pushed Lindsey back on the bed.

BEEP BEEP BEEP. Lindsey's alarm sounded and her eyes shot open guiltily. Had anyone been watching? She looked around frantically for a moment, then sank back on her towel, laughing. The fantasy was intense, but it was in her head, private. Even if her nipples were a little harder than usual. Well, that was the sun and the breeze. She pulled her bathing suit up over the telltale nipples. Enough sun for today. She never wanted to burn these tender little things. Never.

"There you are. I thought I'd never find you."

Angie groaned at the sound of Ellen's voice and rolled over, her broad back radiating irritation.

"What are you doing way up here in the dunes? Isn't it too hot up here, I mean the breeze never penetrates, never, but maybe it is a little too chilly down further today. I've seen some clouds going over." The monologue paused for a moment as a short, stocky woman with a baby-chubby face dumped a cooler, large towel, and backpack in a pile in the sand. "Hey, Lisa," she shouted, turning to wave to a figure several blankets away, "they're over here. I found them."

"Well," she flounced her towel out flat, eyed the sun to make sure she'd gotten the right angle, then flopped down with a sigh of exhaustion. She brushed her dark curly hair out with her fingers and shook her head experimentally. She seemed to be satisfied with how she looked.

"Hi, Lindsey. Hi, Angie. God, what a gruesome rehearsal. I can't believe we're going to open this show in five short nights. Harvey would croak if he could see us now, just croak, don't you know?"

"Hi, Ellen," Lindsey said, raising her head a couple of inches to look over Ellen's way. "I'm sure *Torch Song* has survived many incarnations and probably won't croak from this one. Michael giving you problems again?"

Michael was the director of Provincetown's only live summer theater, and Ellen was his producer, prop man, costume advisor, and all-round coach. Lindsey, Angie, Lisa, and other occasional roommates had been hearing Ellen's complaints for two solid weeks. She'd been thrilled to come out to the Cape for this professional theater job for about ten minutes, or so it seemed to her listeners, and it had been downhill from there.

"I just don't understand why he couldn't find a Jewish faggot to play Norman. Is that too much to ask? I mean, today I am trying to teach this goy how to say *mazel tov* like he doesn't have a mouth full of white bread."

Angie hadn't budged since Ellen's arrival, and she didn't seem inclined to socialize just now.

"How did you ever get Lisa to come to the beach?" Lindsey asked, propping herself up on one elbow to get a view of Lisa who was kneeling down at a blanket half obscured by the dune. "She always laughs at us white girls out here getting suntans and skin cancer."

"I think there's another interest," Ellen offered, the warm sun and soft breeze finally seeming to calm her. "Some dykes from Trinidad hit these shores yesterday, and Lisa's been stalking them all morning. If she found them, that's the last we'll see of her for a while. I've been following leads for her these last two hours." She spoke without rancor, as if she'd been glad to be of use.

Angie roused herself at this information and cast a curious glance in Lisa's direction. That's it, Lindsey realized. Angie and Lisa weren't lovers, but they were long-time friends, and Angie was jealous of Ellen. Lisa had fallen into an easy friendship with Ellen, even though they'd only known each other a few weeks. Ellen was a "helper" around the house, around town. If she took you on, there was nothing she wouldn't do for you. Ellen had taken Lisa on, and it seemed to be O.K. with Lisa. So Angie was jealous, Lindsey mused again. Oh, it wasn't that Ellen couldn't be irritating at times, Lindsey reminded herself, doing her frequent mental self-correction, but she'd thought it was more than irritation from living so closely—the four of them in the tiny two-bedroom house.

Still ignoring Ellen, Angie began to smear some more suntan oil on her huge breasts. "So is that all you're going to tell me about last night, Lindsey?"

"OOOh, what happened last night?" Ellen's languor had been quite temporary, and she turned toward Lindsey expectantly, propping her chin on her fists in an attitude that made her look like a slightly darker, less naive Shirley Temple.

Lindsey thought for a moment, her head tilted to one side. She wanted to seem fairly casual about this, sophisticated, like she did one-night stands whenever the spirit moved her. But still, she needed a little more information. Angie had spent three summers on the Cape and seemed to know the history of every dyke and most of the faggots who had ever visited.

"Do you know her? Her name is Ra."

"Oh, yeah." Angie stressed the *yeah* and looked impressed. "She with her group?"

"She was with two other women. What do you mean, *group?*" They had all been attractive, sophisticated women in their mid-thirties or early forties. Lindsey had assumed the other two were a couple, since that was how most women came to P-town.

"They're an item." Angie looked pleased with herself for having this information available. "You know, a ménage à trois." She could see Lindsey wasn't getting it. "They're all lovers together, Lindsey. Sometimes one of them splits off and cruises, sometimes another, but they always go back to the ménage."

"You're kidding?" Lindsey couldn't think of anything else to say. It had never occurred to her to ask Ra *that*. In fact, she hadn't asked her much of anything. One slow dance at the bar, that anticipatory walk down Commercial Street to her room. What had they talked about? "But she's a teacher."

Ellen snorted a short laugh.

"Yeah. So?" Angie's voice was patient. "It's not something you put on a resume, is it? One of them is a stockbroker; the other is a psychologist with a private practice in Boston. They're discrete, you know. I keep hearing rumors one of them is going into politics." Angie shifted her large, oiled body into a new position on the blanket. "I'm impressed, kid. Not bad for your first summer." She looked like she was about to fade out again, then suddenly hoisted up on her elbows and peered at Lindsey over her sunglasses.

"So, did you do safe sex?"

"Oh, Angie, spare us. We all know you're an AIDS trainer in your real life." Ellen sat up and looked around. "I'm going to see if Lisa found what she was looking for." She hoisted herself to her feet, lifted her bathing suit straps back up over her shoulders, and flounced off.

"We talked about it, Angie, actually." Lindsey wasn't sure she wanted to have this conversation either and was tempted to follow Ellen. Angie could be difficult, but for three summers now Angie'd had control of renting out the house they were living in. It was one of the best deals in P-town, so mostly it was smart not to rock the boat with her.

"TALKED ABOUT IT? What does that do for you? I'm talking about protecting yourself when you're out there being Ms. Hot Stuff. It's one thing to say yes to whatever comes down the road, but, I mean, did you DO safe sex? Ellen can be blasé about this stuff, but I know too much. And I'm concerned about you."

"Calm down, Angie." Lindsey thought her intensity was a little overplayed, even for someone who did AIDS training in the Boston high schools during the year. She hoped, not for the first time in the three short weeks she'd known Angie, that this interest in her was strictly that of a concerned friend, not someone who was going to want to "explore their mutual sexual vibrations," as she'd heard Angie put it last week. Lindsey was sure there were no vibrations for her at all when she looked at Angie. True, she admired how Angie liked herself the way she was, wasn't ashamed to be seen on the beach, and all that. But Lindsey harbored a vague and unexamined suspicion that she could never be attracted to someone like Angie, someone the world would call fat.

Lindsey made her voice light and joking when she answered. "There was no blood, Angie, you'll be glad to hear, nor did I ingest any dangerous bodily fluids. So relax."

BEEP BEEP BEEP. It was Lindsey's watch again. Time to head back to the apartment and get ready for another evening of waiting on tables. And more than that now, Lindsey realized. Another evening of waiting to see who walked through the door of the Safe Harbor. She gathered up her towel, shook it out, and stuffed it in her backpack. She set her watch for 3:45, the moment she had to walk out of the apartment in order to be at work on time. Then she grabbed her sneakers and bike helmet.

"See you later," she said to Angie's prone back.

Pedaling to town, standing under the stinging shower spray, Lindsey considered what Angie had told her about Ra. *Ménage à trois*. She rolled the words around on her tongue. What did it mean? How did they do it? She remembered Ra's expert hands on her body. She had been experienced, that was for sure.

Lindsey wished Sheila were here. Reliable Sheila, her best friend, confidante, advisor. Sheila, source of all necessary but obscure information. Sheila, who had an opinion about everything that ever had happened or might happen. Sheila, who never laughed at you. She could have told Sheila about Ra. Figured out what she was feeling now. Was it shame? Had she been really dumb? Or was it just a normal thing, one of those things that women did all the time when they were making love?

"Hey, slow down a minute, sweetie." Ra's voice had been sort of amused, but that hand that gripped Lindsey's wrist left no room for argument.

Later Lindsey remembered that Ra had said she was a teacher. It fit. There was authority in her voice as well as kindness when she took Lindsey through it. She had said something about focusing, but what Lindsey remembered was the moment when Ra switched on the light, bringing their two naked bodies into full view. She had reached over to the bedside table for something—Lindsey was still blinking in the brighter light—and, still holding Lindsey's wrist, began filing her fingernail. Oh, it had been sensual enough. Kisses between each finger, some massage, and Ra's joking made it seem O.K. at the time.

But god, Lindsey wondered, rinsing the soap out of her long brown hair, did I really hurt her? How awful. It hadn't seemed like such hot sex right then, no matter what Angie thought. Then Ra had taken Lindsey's hand and led it down to her cunt again, spread her legs in the light and let Lindsey's hand rest on the mound of her pubis. That was when the lesson had come. Lindsey had to admit she'd been fascinated. Ra's pubic hair was thick and honey-colored, darker than the ash blonde shading her temples. Ra's hands spread the lips of her cunt wide and her voice invited Lindsey to stroke the clitoris, move slowly from the wet dark opening up to the shell-pink little button hiding under the soft fleshy hood. Ra was turned on—Lindsey could hear the tremor in her voice as she gave instructions. She followed the pace Ra set, followed the slow voice at first in her stroking, then moving faster as Ra became more urgent, her back arching, her cunt pushing up into Lindsey's hand.

"A little harder now," Ra panted. She was still trying for control, Lindsey realized, as Ra's hips writhed beneath her hand. Sitting cross-legged on the bed next to Ra, Lindsey could see Ra's whole body. The small well-defined breasts rode high on her chest and her ribs were just visible under strong muscles. Letting her one hand follow Ra's rhythm, Lindsey began to stroke lightly with her other, up the belly first, then to the bottom cup of one breast, then the other. Ra's eyes were finally closed as she went inward to concentrate. Lindsey pinched lightly the nipple of the breast she had been rubbing. "Harder," Ra gasped. Harder where? Lindsey wondered. She kept pinching the nipple that was getting smaller and firmer under her fingers. Suddenly Ra's knees jerked, and Lindsey felt the orgasm starting under her fingers. She rubbed Ra's clitoris until she was sure she'd gone over the edge, then let her fingers burrow into Ra's wet center and catch at the waves of orgasm pulsing down her abdomen.

"Whew." Lindsey broke the fantasy by stepping out of the shower; she realized she'd been standing in the pounding water for a long, long time. Maybe it had been good sex. Hot sex. They'd both had orgasms, that was for sure. And when Ra asked Lindsey, "Do you want me to walk you home?" Lindsey was relieved. They were cuddling under a sheet, back in the candlelight now, letting the shadows play over them as they rubbed and fondled, but she was ready to leave, ready to find her own bed for a few hours, ready for some solitude while she figured out what had just happened and how she felt about it.

Maybe it would be a quiet night tonight. Lindsey grabbed the murder mystery she'd been trying to get into all week and shoved it in her pack. Angie, Ellen, Ellen's lover Nutmeg, they'd all read it on the beach and told her it was *important* and fun. All about the antiporn/pro-SM fights going on somewhere. Lindsey didn't know much about that, but so far the book had been a lot of argument about ideas and no sex at all. Weird. She'd thought the book was going to be about sex.

Back on her bike, pedaling the wrong way down Commercial Street toward Safe Harbor, Lindsey let her brown hair stream out wetly behind her. By the time she got to the restaurant it would be dry and she could braid it in one long heavy braid and tie it with her lavender ribbon. Ra had untied the braid while they'd danced and spread Lindsey's hair like silk across her shoulders. Lindsey had felt the eyes of several women looking at her from the dark edges of Mizmoon's dance floor as she and Ra flirted sensuously, their intentions obvious to them—and to anyone who saw them, Lindsey imagined. She'd found it an incredible turn-on, playing like that, saying with her body to Ra, to herself, to anyone watching, *Hey, I'm going to have sex with this woman.* As she slow-danced, breast to breast with Ra, Lindsey took two long strands of her hair and brought them together at the nape of Ra's neck. "Got you," she'd mocked, "got you all tied up."

"That's fine with me, Lindsey," Ra had purred in her ear. "That's just fine with me."

A loud horn shocked Lindsey out of her fantasy. Her eyes jerked sideways just as a heavy-duty black pickup began accelerating toward her. Lindsey braked and swerved in the gravel driveway she'd been crossing. "Whyntcha go somewheres else to kill yerself?" screamed the driver, as he gunned the shiny black-and-chrome truck out into Commercial Street, scattering pedestrians, narrowly missing the horse and buggy parked by the curb.

Lindsey drew a deep breath and pulled her other leg off, over the bike. She wasn't hurt. Thank god she didn't go down in the gravel. What an asshole. She shrugged her shoulders and decided—still shaky—to walk the block and a half to work.

She'd heard this was a rough week. It was the last weekend in June, the final week before the unofficial gay season started. Sunday morning was the "blessing of the fleet." A real scene, according to Angie. The last gasp of the hets. Every sailor on the Cape came out for this weekend, and the bishop or some big muckamuck from the church waved incense at the boats and they were ready for the season. Sort of like getting a spiritual caulking, Angie said, so they could get through the summer without springing leaks. Lindsey thought the idea was kind of nice, but she didn't like what went with it—lots of drinking macho sailors. She hoped there wouldn't be too many of them at Safe Harbor tonight. She'd looked for a restaurant where she could work with other queers, but not one of the upscale places where a family with kids wouldn't feel comfortable.

"Hey, Lin, wait up," a voice hailed her from behind. Danny. That must mean she wasn't late for work at any rate.

"How was your date, sweetie? You sure finished your tables in a hurry. She'd have waited a little longer for you, you know. I saw her out there, pretending to be interested in Teenage Mutant Ninja Turtle T-shirts and designer sunglasses in that awful display window."

Lindsey blushed first, then started to giggle. "God, Danny, you don't miss anything, do you?"

Danny reminded Lindsey of her next oldest brother Carl back in Illinois. Danny seemed to know her without having to know her, just like Carl had never needed to ask where she'd been or what she was doing to understand how she was feeling and what was going on with her. Carl was the only one of her three brothers and two sisters she'd come out to. She hadn't, actually. He'd known. She came home from college that third summer and been moody, removed from the family but desperate to be with them all. Maybe Carl had seen her walk out to the mailbox three or four times in the morning before the mail could possibly have been delivered; maybe he'd known she was getting a letter a day from Belle all during June. And after that, when the letters stopped coming, maybe he'd heard her crying at night, sitting in the swing on the dark front porch, not wanting to be inside where the rest of them were watching TV, not really wanting to be alone, either.

"Why don't you tell me about her?" he'd finally asked, moving to sit with her as she sat and swung back and forth, back and forth, the summer waning and the reality of a year of college—her last— looming ahead without Belle, facing her squarely.

Danny seemed to know Lindsey like that, know her from their first meeting, know her beyond the things she was willing to say about herself, beyond the mask she hoped she had created of a happy-go-lucky, summer off from grad school, pretty experienced dyke of the world. It worked with her housemates. But not with Danny. He knew about masks. Told her about them the first night they'd worked together, a long slow night midweek when Lindsey found it hard to believe Safe Harbor could even survive financially, let alone need to hire her.

"Everybody comes out here to be somebody they can't be anywhere else," Danny explained. "Sometimes it's really their only chance to be openly gay. Is that a mask, or is the life they lead the rest of the year the mask? I'm never sure. But lot's of times people come here to be somebody they've imagined, somebody they'd like to be but can't be at home. In a way, you know, it's a drag on creativity, being known. Out here I can be a muscle man in a jockstrap one day, a sissy waiting for my dream-hunk-stud the next. Who cares what my name is or how I got here or where I'll go when the summer ends? But back at grad school I'm Daniel Stein who always gets A+ and is a nice Jewish boy from the Bronx. I could walk back into my MBA program with this haircut, but what's the point if everybody knows me the way I've always been. People don't like to let you change. It upsets the balance."

Lindsey watched Danny choreograph his words with his hands and arms and doubted that he'd ever experienced a drag on his creativity. Upsetting other people's balances, yes, she could imagine that. That first night he'd had a crew cut, long and spiky with mousse and a little pigtail coming down behind his ear. Rimless round glasses sat prissily on his nose, and he wore a blue workshirt open down most of the front to make sure no one missed his absolutely perfect chest, his sleek, muscled, and gorgeously tanned physique.

After a few nights Lindsey realized Danny's description of the self behind that mask was another mask, but gradually he lifted enough layers of disguise for her to think she knew him. There was more to

Daniel Stein than the "nice Jewish boy" routine. That facade hid the years he'd spent escaping his too-good-to-be-true image—a life drenched in alcohol and drugs, lost to himself but safe from the life of a straight, upstanding Jewish male he thought was trying to claim him back home. And now there was the Danny trying to make restitution by working in recovery groups. Trying to talk with his father, to make a future in spite of the lost dreams. And the Danny who still didn't understand why it had gone wrong in the first place, who couldn't make sense of it at all. And what would be behind that Danny, Lindsey wondered.

"You're kind of sad, aren't you?" he'd asked that first night, his head tilted to one side, the waving choreography halted in midair for a moment. "Oh, I know, you've got yourself up like a P-town dyke out to cruise."

Lindsey flushed and lowered her head with anger. She wasn't going to talk like this with a stranger, a man at that. So what if Angie and Ellen had helped her decide which silk shirt to wear for this first night at work, how to choose a different earring for each ear lobe.

Danny put a comforting hand on Lindsey's shoulder. "I *try* to look like Arsenio Hall crossed with a Girl Scout camp counselor, so I know when I meet a sister in disguise."

In spite of herself, Lindsey was laughing. Wholesome was not a disguise for her. That was what she was trying to escape. Or thought she was. Along with the sadness that had ridden on her shoulder all through this first year of grad school, the sadness that kept saying, *This isn't right for you.* But she couldn't hear any voices telling her what was right. She wondered if she was as transparent to the world as she seemed to be to Danny.

Danny said he'd come to P-town looking for himself. "Lots of us do. It's a place where, since we don't have to try and be gay, we can try and be whatever *else* it is we need to be." She hoped he was right. Being a lesbian wasn't her issue, she insisted to herself, to Sheila, to anyone who would listen. But she didn't know what her issue was.

They had only worked together for three weeks, but now Lindsey walked comfortably next to Danny, wheeling her bike in and out of the tourists clogging the street. "Nice outfit, Heidi," she commented, eyeing his scarlet silk shirt. "Kind of out of character for you, isn't it?"

"Sweetie, it's my roommate's pajama top. I just couldn't resist. Is
it too not me, do you think?" Danny's hands caressed his silken chest,
fluttered out into the air.

"Who are you, Danny?" Lindsey shrugged. "It's a gorgeous shirt.
Just like something I might wear, that's all."

"Oh, well, don't define your style by making it not-Danny." All
of a sudden his voice sounded irritable to Lindsey, and she looked
at him sharply.

She was feeling irritable herself, still off balance from the shock of
nearly being run down by that jerk in a pickup truck. The sun was
so bright it washed color out of the sky, out of the tourists' garish
T-shirts. Lindsey wasn't looking forward to spending the next eight
hours working in this stifling heat.

In the shift of a moment, the weekend stretching ahead of her
seemed long and slightly sinister. The heat rose from the street, from
the docks, from the decks of the ships gathered in the harbor. Call
it the blessing of the fleet, call it community ritual, to Lindsey it
seemed like the effect was to declare open season on anyone who was
different, anyone who was outside that old definition of being "like
us."

Every year, Angie said, there'd been at least a couple of incidents
of fag and dyke bashing, especially at this time of year. It was the dark
side of this town of sun-drenched beaches and sun-washed streets.
At night those beaches were shrouded in darkness, Lindsey remembered, lit only occasionally by the lighthouses' sweeping beams.

Chapter Two

That *was* the way my third week in P-town started. Friday night had brought me Ra, and Saturday was only half-started when I had to negotiate how much to tell Angie about Friday night and was nearly run down by a crazy truck driver on my way to work. I was not looking forward to the rest of Saturday, I can tell you, and then to find Danny in a snit as well. What am I doing here? is a question I have asked myself many times in this life. That night was no exception. And probably I was most off center because I really didn't know if I wanted to see Ra again or not, but I caught myself looking for her everywhere I went. Maybe I just wanted a glimpse of her, or wanted to check her out with her two lovers. I confess—I wanted to know what a ménage à trois looked like from the outside, and I hadn't really focused on the question, as it were, when I was waiting on their table Friday night.

Danny was right when he said we come to P-town to just *be* gay and find whatever else it is we need to know about ourselves. Being a lesbian wasn't the main thing on my mind that summer. I was looking for a life direction—more even than a career. I wanted to work at something I cared about passionately. And with more independence, less supervision, than my dead-end jobs had provided. Grad school seemed an obvious direction last year, but by spring I didn't feel a master's degree in social work would take me anywhere I wanted to go.

How did I get to P-town? This doesn't make a whole lot of sense to me now, but I think I told myself that if I couldn't figure out what

I wanted to do with my work life, maybe I could at least be swept off my feet by love. Passion comes in different forms, and if I couldn't have any in my work life, well, I guessed I'd settle for it in my love life. Like it was easy to find. And like I could be sure I'd recognize it when it happened. Which is probably why I was so tense on Saturday night, trying to figure out how to *classify* what had happened with Ra, then decide if I wanted a repeat.

So I ignored Danny and stomped into the restaurant and started my setups. My adrenalin was still hyper from the close call with the truck in the afternoon. At least that's what I told myself when I knocked over the third saltshaker. But that wasn't why I looked up every time the door opened. The question was how should I act if they, the three of them, came in again? Would they all know about last night? What had she told them about me? What if Ra came in alone, or—this one sent my adrenalin right back up there—what if she came in with someone new? Another pickup for the evening.

I do this all the time. My brain has an automatic on switch for questions, but I've never figured out where the off button is.

"Stop with the questions," Sheila would tell me. "It's not like you ask real questions that have answers. You have all these 'what ifs.' Nobody could answer the questions you ask."

She's right, I know she is, but that never seemed to stop the questions. I look at it this way: if you can't imagine something in advance, how can you possibly cope with it when it happens? Like I *had* to figure out the best way to act if Ra waltzed in here with another woman for the evening, right? Wrong. Sheila's voice came right back at me, "Did you imagine going home with her last night before it happened? Or was it a miracle and you acted spontaneously?"

I met Sheila the first day of grad school. We'd both been out working in the field for a few years. I noticed her in class right away when she used her experience as an alcoholism counselor for juveniles as the basis for asking a question. I'd been a childcare worker in a semi-lockup for teenage girls, so I knew what she was talking about. I might not have been so willing to connect with her, though, if I'd realized at the beginning that Sheila always had an opinion about everything, and usually her opinion and the instructor's weren't the same. She was too controversial for me to feel comfortable with.

And talk about letting people know your business. There was nothing Sheila wouldn't say. Or so I thought at first. We learned she was a recovering alcoholic herself in "Special Problems in Social Work." In "Marriage and the Family" she came out as a lesbian. We learned about her ex-husband who was a batterer toward the end of that semester. And when "Child Development" started—you guessed it— Sheila told us about her childhood sexual abuse.

"It's too bad she's not overweight and crippled," I heard one of the pimple-plagued juveniles quip on the way out of class, "then she'd have one of everything we're studying." It wasn't the first time there'd been comments like that about her. Maybe I'd even groaned with the rest of them when she'd started her most recent question with, "As a recovering survivor of childhood sexual abuse..."

One day in the cafeteria, Sheila nailed me as I opened my bag lunch. "Why are you avoiding me, Lindsey?" she wanted to know. I choked on my egg salad sandwich and began to protest, but she cut me off.

"You've had enough experience to know what's happening." Sheila was intense, and her dark eyes narrowed as she forced me to look at her directly for the first time in weeks. I was reluctant to admit I didn't know what was happening, so I shrugged, trying to appear noncommittal.

"They're afraid. They don't want to know this stuff is real, that it happens to real people. But you've been out there. You've seen kids who've been abused. Why aren't you supporting me?"

"What should I support? I don't like classes that turn into team sports. You know, with winners and losers. I like to listen, have time to take it in and think about it. Then I decide whether I agree or not. I put my opinions in my papers," I added defensively.

"Then I guess it's all abstract for you, huh? It doesn't hit you where you live." Sheila gestured vigorously at her solar plexus.

"It's true I don't come from a broken or abusive family. I'm not an addict. In fact, I consider myself fairly normal." I was hedging nervously now.

"Hmpf." Sheila was thinking very carefully before her next assault, I could tell.

"Are you a lesbian?"

Shit. It was a direct question. The kind I tried never to hedge. I don't think we can get very far if we deny who we are. And besides, it feels shitty saying, "Oh, gosh, no," and leaving other people out there to take the risks. Sometimes my training gets in my way. I mean, the training I got being a women's studies major. We were taught about feminist standards and feminist ethics, and leaving a sister alone to take the heat was something you just didn't do. According to my earnest and intelligent (and sometimes gorgeous) women profs, anyway.

Why hadn't she just said, "Oh, gee, I thought you were a lesbian," or something like that? And I could have said, "Oh, yeah?" and excused myself and gone to the library. I know, I know, it's pretty close to the same thing. But not quite. So relax. I confessed.

"Yeah, I am," I said in my you-wanna-make-somethin-of-it voice. "But I don't think it keeps me from being normal."

"Ah, ha." Sheila looked as though she had discovered a rare secret in her tupperware bowl of salad. "Then you're out to your family— the whole happy extended lot of them—and you were out on the job when you worked with those teenage girls and, let's see," she paused for breath, "oh, yes, out to all your professors here and classmates. Do you go to church? Of course if you do you're out there, too, right? And it's fine with all of them. Never had a problem, huh?" She smiled triumphantly. "I've been waiting for years to meet a lesbian who was perfectly normal."

"Sheila, I said I'm a normal enough person, not that I live in a perfect world." My irritation was barely suppressed.

"Not possible." She waved her fork in the air as she made this pronouncement. "The world won't let you be normal, don't you know that? Besides," she gave a thin conspiratorial smile, "you're better than normal. Why would *you* ever want to settle for normal?"

I confess, she got me with that appeal to my. . .well, to my vanity. It was harder to dismiss her as a crank after that, and soon we were wrangling our way through those long Monday, Wednesday, and Friday lunches like aging sparring partners. One of the first things I learned from Sheila was that people who seem to be very open about their private business may just be constructing a mask, a facade behind which they can live. From her point of view, the things she talked about in class were the easy things. They kept her from seeming mysterious, she said, and let her live with her real secrets. I had to admit the truth of what she was saying. I knew Sheila was a lesbian, but I had no idea who her lover was or if she had one or none or many. I'd guessed she was Jewish, but it was something I never heard her refer to in public. I knew she was divorced, but I didn't learn for months that she had a daughter, and then I was only allowed to know that because I'd become a friend. Family was a very private matter with Sheila.

So we talked from December until May when I was ready to take off for my summer-job-and-rest-camp. About March I realized I was talking to Sheila even when she wasn't around. It gave me a way of controlling those voices a little. Sheila was a skeptic. She didn't buy anybody's mythology. Her voice didn't stop my self-questioning, but it gave me some perspective on it. On a good day.

By the time I finished setting up all eight of my tables, I was sort of hoping for a busy night. And not just because of the tips: there's less time to think when you're in motion.

Just then the door opened. My head jerked up, pulse started to race, the whole nine yards. Walter, the manager, escorted a man and woman and two under-six children to one of my tables. I took a deep breath, shuddered with relief, and went over to take their orders. I could tell it was going to be that kind of a night.

I didn't even know Ra's last name. Irrelevant. I should start with the basics. I didn't know if I wanted a repeat of last night. I wasn't sure my nerves, or my self-esteem, could stand it.

I delivered three Cokes and a Miller Lite to my table and started reciting the specials. I got as far as the clambake when my mind flipped back to me delivering the order of steamers to Ra's table last night, then to looking for her little morsel under the glare of the bedroom's harsh overhead light. I was standing there with my mouth open, staring at these people sitting at my table like they had just walked in from another planet.

"That's O.K." The daddy took advantage of my unnatural pause. "I think we just want three fish-and-chip platters. The kids will split one if you'll bring a fourth plate."

I nodded mutely and fled.

As you may have noticed, I am a person who wants a certain

amount of control in my life. I expect to have the ability to behave
well in public. It was a family badge of honor, our bottom line, in
other jargon. My parents were teachers, Methodists, community pil-
lars who cared what the neighbors thought in our little suburb of
Evanston, Illinois. If you care what the neighbors think, you'd better plan on having a good supply of self-control, as well as control
over circumstances some people never think about, like choosing a
neat, respectable career, living in neighborhoods where surprises don't
happen, that kind of thing. As far as I was concerned, being a lesbian took me as far away from Evanston as I wanted to go. I'm a dyke,
I told myself, not a rebel. That was before I learned there was only
so far I could walk down that road until I found myself not making
any sense at all. It's funny how holding on to control, or what feels
like control, can spin you far enough out from the center that you
wonder if you'll ever recover.

So I was grateful trade picked up, even when it got hectic, obnoxious, and tiring. Because I wasn't *even* in control of my thoughts, not
at all. I felt like the dirty old rag our family dog liked to pick up and
shake and shake. I was a boat knocked loose from its mooring, and
about a dozen other clichés all at once. It was an anxiety attack of
major proportions.

No surprise that I overreacted at the end of the evening when
Danny stopped me at the bar and whispered his idea of a hot item
in my ear.

"She's a WHAT?"

"Cool it, Lindsey. You'll blow my tip." Danny looked anxiously over
his shoulder. "I saw you cruising her, so I thought I'd fill you in. For-
get I said anything." He tossed his pigtail over his shoulder with a
shake of his head and started for the other end of the bar.

"Danny, you ass," I hissed at him, "get back here and tell me what
you heard or I'll never tell you another single thing about my life."

"Oh, god, what a threat." His voice went nasal and his wrist limp.

"Never mind. I don't want to know." I turned to face the bartender,
wishing he'd hurry with the three margaritas for my table. I hated
it when Danny did that. I could never tell who he was mocking—
himself, effeminate men, or the stereotypical woman, but I was tired
of arguing with him about it. And he wasn't the least bit interested

in what we said in "Intro to Feminism" about gay men who mock women's femininity and its connection to misogyny.

In fact, I was rather tired of this whole evening. If he'd given me another minute, I could have worked up a good tired with this whole Cape deal. And especially tired of—

"Sorry, love. You've had a heavy night tonight. Some of those tables have been a bitch." His voice was concerned, his face contrite.

He redeemed himself. I accepted his apology and took my drinks from the bartender. *Bitch* barely described the last foursome of drunken fraternity guys trying to impress an older group of three weekend sailors from Boston. All trying to out "big-better-best" one another. My only hope had been to let them know I wasn't part of their audience, but that didn't matter much since they were performing for one another.

"The myth of heterosexuality," I reported to Danny during one breather, "is alive and well. They only pretend they're doing that for women, don't they?"

And then two women came in and told us they'd witnessed a truckful of teenagers drench two women walking arm in arm down Commercial Street. The teens had yelled and catcalled, the usual harassment, but as the women tried to dodge back out of the way, one of the boys had dumped a bucket of something on the women, probably sea water or sewage. "It smelled terrible," the older of these two women said heatedly. "The whole thing was just disgusting."

Walter asked if they had called the police, but these two witnesses hadn't and they didn't know if the women who were attacked had reported it, although several women had gone to assist them, they said. "We would have gone over, too, but there were plenty of people helping out and sometimes you can just be in the way."

Walter went to the phone to make sure somebody had reported this. It wasn't the first time in these three weeks I'd seen him make that call. Too many incidents like this get glossed over, he told me when I started working, or never make it to a police report because people are afraid to get involved.

I served some more drinks, wondering as I thought about the story of this attack what color truck these teenagers had been driving. In my mind's eye I could still see the black fender and shiny chrome of the pickup that had nearly run me down that afternoon. It was an image that was not going to go away in a hurry.

Finally I got a break between customers' demands and waited at the bar for Danny to come over.

"What do you mean she's a nun, Danny?" For that was the hot tip he'd whispered in my ear twenty minutes ago. I looked over at Danny's last table. It was late and things were finally slowing down. Those three women had come in late and stayed quite a while now. I'd checked them out when they first arrived, remembering what Angie said about Ra and company, curious if threesomes were a usual mode here in P-town. But except for noticing that the youngest of them seemed really cute—in a wholesome sort of way, not like Ra's sophisticated glow last night—I hadn't really had time to even give them my usual careful once-over.

"Go listen," Danny urged. He nodded toward the counter just behind their table, partially hidden by a mirror angled slightly into the room to give the sense of more space than there really was. It was our secret listening post when we wanted to overhear the gossip at one of those tables without being noticed.

I picked up my book of tabs for the evening, and a pencil, and moved back behind the counter. I needed to finish my last two checks anyway and add up the ones from earlier on. And I always check myself for major disasters before I turn the thing into the manager.

The older woman was talking. I started chewing on my pencil stub in mock concentration. She was kind of striking looking, actually. Black, short, straight hair with streaks of silver in it. Dark black eyes. Bet they could look right through you. Now maybe *she* was a nun, but not the other two. No way.

"Believe it. Why can't you believe it? They were lovers for more than thirty years. Wherever Noreen went, Beatrice followed."

"But that doesn't make them *lovers*," protested Wholesome. "I know you weren't even supposed to have 'special friends' back in those days. How do you know they weren't just . . . friends?"

"From the intensity, for one thing." Dark Eyes was pretty intense herself, I can tell you, and I gave up the pretense of addition. Hmm. Each of these women wore a ring on her left hand, third finger. Unless they were married to one another, Danny might be right.

"You should have been around for some of the fights," laughed the third woman, a slightly built, middle-aged brunette with shoulder-length curly hair. "Especially after Noreen got to be Major Superior and started attracting some much younger special friends."

Dark Eyes nodded agreement. "If they had only been friends, the Order could have dealt with it differently. But because they were lovers, everyone had to look the other way. To have confronted it at all would have been scandalous."

"And to have confronted it," inserted Curly Hair, "would have endangered all the *other* couples."

"Right. I always said we should do a sequel to *Lesbian Nuns*, but ours would tell the whole truth." Dark Eyes smiled at Wholesome. "We could call it *Secret Loves at the Provincial House.*

"No, no. Our title is *Out of the Habit*, remember?" Curly Hair paused. "Or was it *Into the Habit?*"

They all laughed. I chewed on my pencil stub some more. Life was never dull here in P-town. Danny was right. Nuns. I wondered why Wholesome seemed more uncomfortable than her friends. She was younger, closer to my age, built like an athlete. A swimmer maybe, with that shaggy, short-cropped haircut. I wondered what color her eyes were. I wondered how long she'd been a nun. And how long she'd been a lesbian. And how many women was it possible for one Lindsey Carter to be *seriously* attracted to in one short weekend. I added that to my list of questions as I walked back over to join Danny at the bar.

"So. You can say, 'I told you so.' " I believe in giving credit where credit is due.

"Is it the blondes you like or the threesomes, do you think?" Danny was peering at me now like I was his specimen for the evening.

I started to react with anger, then laughed. "Don't know. Do you like men who are shorter than you or only the ones who are too busy to see you for more than ten minutes at a time?" Danny had a history of unavailable lovers, men who dashed into his life for a few minutes of his time, then dashed off again to some new project. Sometimes Danny was devastated, sometimes amused, sometimes so busy with his own projects he hardly seemed to notice someone had been and gone.

Danny shrugged. "Probably it's some combination of the two. Lust is a psychological as well as a physical phenomenon, don't you think?"

"I'm not sure I know much about lust," I countered. "I think lust is something male novelists made up. Gay male novelists, maybe. Women experience sexual attraction as a by-product of *love*." There. That was a new dig since Feminism 101. I was laughing now. We were recycling an argument we'd started the first night we met, playing with half-truths like they were hockey pucks or tennis balls as we circled the real quarry, those great gaping unknowns—sex and lust.

"That must be true," Danny admitted coyly. "I saw how you developed a firm friendship with her last night as the basis for a long and enduring relationship before you snuck out of here for a quick fuck."

"Ahhh, yes." Danny was sharp. It made it worth playing the game with him. But I wasn't sure I wanted to be reminded of that just now. For I had no well-constructed explanations, no theories from any class I'd ever taken that would get me from the beginning to the end of last night with all of my preconceptions intact. And I'm pretty fond of some of my preconceptions.

Walter was laughing and shaking his head at us. Sometimes he looked like he wanted to play, too, but he found it too hard to jump in. Danny liked to use Walter against me—Walter and William, the perfect couple, the ideal of permanence in a constantly fluctuating stream of transient one-night stands, quick fucks in the back of the bar or bathhouse. In the Age of AIDS, as Danny says, gay men need their Walter and Williams, just like dykes need something to overcome their staidness, their image of warm, huggy domesticity and no sex, lust, or passion.

I was going to tell Danny I was just fulfilling my community obligation to give dykes a new image of ourselves, to affirm our right to say yes to our lust, but he had waltzed off to see what the nuns wanted at his table. My last customers were stirring like they'd be ready for their checks soon. I bent over the counter and started to add them up.

"Excuse me."

Slightly irritated at the interruption, I turned and looked over my shoulder, one finger marking my place on the pad of figures.

Green, I realized with a shock. Her eyes were green.

"I really like your hair. Have you ever cut it?" Wholesome the nun smiled at me, her green eyes crinkling around the edges. Moonlight on still ocean water, the image floated in front of my eyes, and I could hear the sound of the lonesome foghorn moaning offshore, I swear to you.

"Uhhh, no. I mean, yes." Talk mouth, I commanded myself, trying desperately for control, trying to ignore Danny's bemused looks as he piled dirty dishes on a tray.

"It was cut once when I was little, but I've never let it be cut since I had control of those sorts of things." I stammered a little as I got that out and then tried to think of something else to say.

"I just wondered, since I . . . mine was never cut until . . ." Wholesome paused, and I wondered what she wanted to conceal. ". . .Until a couple of years ago. I really like yours." She smiled and gave a half wave as she moved to join her two friends at the door.

I turned back toward the bar, hoping to hide my awkwardness. I couldn't help but hear Wholesome's two friends congratulate her as she left the restaurant. "Way to go, *Carol*. You may be ready for Lesson Four in the *Dyke Cruising Manual*. . . ."

To my relief, their voices faded into the din of Saturday night on a Provincetown street. I stared desperately at my pad, trying to remember what I had been doing two minutes before. I'd had enough. Please. Let it be enough. I wanted to get on my bike and ride home and open a Coke and make some popcorn and curl up with a crossword puzzle. Not even a good book. I wasn't in the mood for a plot tonight, just a few words in a crossword puzzle I could concentrate on to take this overheated brain out of overdrive. More than my brain. My whole body needed a rest.

"Hi, Lindsey," Ra's soft voice caressed my ear. "Thought you might be up for another dance tonight after work."

Chapter Three

Provincetown was humming at eleven o'clock as Lindsey and Ra strolled down Commercial Street toward the pier. People of all descriptions walked down the center of the nearly carless street. Although it was still the night before the blessing of the fleet, it seemed to Lindsey as if a strange and wonderful blending of two cultures had already occurred. Men walked together as couples, arm in arm, women held hands with women, cooed in one another's ears with alarming abandon, while a perfect middle-American family of mommy, daddy, son, and daughter window-shopped with apparently unperturbed attention a few feet away. Several foreign-language conversations mingled with the shouts and laughter of three local preteens trying to guide their skateboards around the tourists.

The speciality shops and souvenir boutiques had all closed, but the bars and clubs were just starting to swing. Ra and Lindsey paused outside a brass-and-leather decor country-western club just before the pier, caught by the sounds of a raunchy, complaining singer wondering where her man had gone.

"I actually kind of like country-western music," Ra said tentatively, looking for Lindsey's response.

"Me, too," Lindsey admitted, "but I don't like the audience." Two men in T-shirts tucked into bluejeans sagging below their beer bellies leaned over the bar nearest them, and several dozen other men were clustered further down. A few couples—men and women couples—sat at tables around the edge of the room.

"If I had a belly like that, I don't think I'd emphasize it with a wide leather belt and a silver-tooled buckle," Ra observed wryly.

"Mmmm." Lindsey nodded agreement. "I've always wondered how they defy gravity like that. I mean, with the pants buckled below the bulge." She shifted uncomfortably. "Of course, not everyone can control their size. There's nothing wrong with being heavier than this crazy society says is attractive."

Ra looked sideways at Lindsey, an amused smile crossing her face, fading, then reappearing. "Let's walk out on the pier," she suggested casually.

Waves slapped drowsily against the pier pilings, and a light mist drifted slowly over the moon, gradually lifting. A tranquil scene, an observer would have said, a calm, slow summer night. No one watching the two women walk under the street lamp and out toward the dark end of the pier could have known whether they were friends or lovers. Their bodies were neither close nor far, revealing no intent beyond watching the moon sink into the water.

"I love the moon like this," Lindsey said, after they'd walked in silence for a moment.

"What do you like about it?" asked Ra quietly, seriously.

"The crescent shape, for one thing. That it's new, for another. And it always seems kind of wonderfully strange that it's setting at this hour. If it were full, it would be over there," she gestured behind them toward the Atlantic, "and it would just be rising."

"The shape reminds me of this."

Ra didn't move quickly, but she took Lindsey's hand and stopped their walk. She bent forward a little, her breath touching Lindsey's cheek like a soft, warm feather, and her tongue traced the rim of Lindsey's ear.

Lindsey shuddered as her breath drew in sharply. Then Ra moved away and the wet crescent on her ear felt cool in the night air.

Lindsey reached for Ra's fingers and twined them in her own as they walked further out on the pier. They were alone in the shadows cast by the moon and mist, the only sound the slap of waves on the boat hulls moored around them and the occasional plaintive hoot of the foghorn.

The two figures paused at the end of the pier. From a distance, an observer could not have known whether they were male or female, young or old, but it would have been clear they were lovers as one figure led the other into a small cul-de-sac away from casual eyes. One figure leaned back, half-sitting on a broad piling, and the other leaned over as if to kiss the upturned face.

"Do you want me to tell you what I'm about to do to you, Lindsey?" Ra purred softly in her tingling ear, "or shall I just do it?"

Do it. The words flew into Lindsey's thoughts, followed immediately by, *Not here.* Ra wasn't exactly waiting for a reply. Her tongue and lips were tracing the outline of Lindsey's jaw, licking and nibbling down toward her neck, now around to the back where her spine was starting to tingle as the hairs stood up in response to her rising pulse, then around to her throat, settling softly on a pulsing artery.

I should tell her to stop was Lindsey's rational thought. What if someone else walked out here? What if some of those het sailors get drunk and come in this direction? She tried to look around Ra's head, but they were surrounded by pilings that created a small but roofless room. And the moon was gone again; they were enveloped in a dark, quiet pocket. That darkness seemed a permission to Lindsey, as if she were in a dream life and the need for control was gone for a moment, faded into the less real, waking life.

"Tell me," a voice that was hers demanded. And she could feel Ra's lips pull into a satisfied smile.

"Mmmm. I'm going to lean you back right here where you're sitting." As she said the words her hands took Lindsey's wrists and moved them behind her so she could brace her weight.

"And I'm going to slide your hips forward so it will be very hard for you to move at all." She did that, her two hands pressing firmly on Lindsey's buttocks, pulling her forward until her legs dangled freely.

"You'll feel very exposed like that," Ra said, running her hand down over Lindsey's belly and crotch.

Lindsey caught her breath sharply, realizing Ra was right. In just a moment she had become more vulnerable. If she wanted to stop Ra now, she would have to make a pronounced effort. She would have to shift her weight and jump down off the piling completely to regain control.

"Then I'm going to loosen your shorts here in front a little," her hands followed her words. "I really like that you don't wear a bra, Lindsey. Your breasts are right here waiting for me and," she trailed her fingers up Lindsey's belly to her nipples, "and, yes, they are waiting." Ra chuckled as her fingers circled Lindsey's taut hard nipples. "I like pinching nipples like these, Lindsey." She was whispering in Lindsey's ear again, her tongue and lips never stopping. "I like pinching them hard and knowing how much they like that. I'm going to pinch them until you feel it all the way down your center. And when you feel it in your clit, then you're going to ask me to touch you there. All you have to do is say one word. *Please.*"

Lindsey whimpered, feeling the wetness melt in her vagina with the expectation Ra's words created in her body. But Ra's mouth covered hers in a long, drowning kiss and she couldn't say the word yet, couldn't move, could only let Ra's fingers massage and pinch and tickle her breasts as the heat rose inside her. Were there other people on the dock? Was there danger lurking in the shadows? Was there pain laced with the sharp pleasure Ra's fingers were giving her? Lindsey didn't know or care.

"Please," she gasped when Ra's mouth pulled away from hers.

And slowly the teasing fingers moved downward. Lindsey's stomach muscles quivered under Ra's touch from the strain of leaning back.

Then Ra lifted Lindsey's shirt and she felt night air on her hot breasts. "I'm going to leave your breasts out here for the moon to admire," she said. "And I'll move these shorts down a little. My, my," she mocked, as her hands pulled Lindsey's shorts from beneath, "you're a little damp there, Lindsey."

Ra stood back from Lindsey suddenly, and Lindsey realized she was sitting in an almost-public place with her breasts and pubic hair exposed, her shorts dangling below her knees, her T-shirt folded up over her shoulders. And her hands weren't even free to cover herself if she'd wanted to.

Ra's eyes were taking in every detail of what she had created. "And now, Lindsey," she paused, waited. Lindsey moaned again softly. "I'm going to lick and nibble your clit until you come and then I'm going to do something else to you, but it will be a surprise. And you're going to stay like that with your breasts smiling up at the moon until I tell you it's all right to move."

Ra knelt, and Lindsey felt her shoulders between her knees, her tongue probing as her fingers parted the lips of Lindsey's vagina. Ra sucked and nibbled, swallowed from Lindsey's smooth wetness, then moved her tongue hard against Lindsey's clitoris, pushing, circling, then pushing again until an orgasm pulsed out of Lindsey's toes, pushing up to her thighs, swelling her cunt, and throbbing finally into her uterus.

But Ra didn't stop. Her mouth moved away and her fingers went into Lindsey's cunt. Two, three, then four fingers stretched her open, and a thumb pressed on her clitoris as Ra's mouth moved up Lindsey's belly and clamped firmly on her breast. Lindsey felt her whole breast sucked into Ra's mouth, felt it press against the back of her throat. Then her breast slipped out of the warm, wet mouth, and the other was engulfed. It was like being swallowed, Lindsey thought, as Ra's fingers opened her cunt wider and wider, moved up and down, moved in deeper, then pulled out, moved in. It was like being swallowed and opened up to the world at the same time. The whole world could be watching now and it wouldn't have mattered. Her vagina had never been so full and then so empty. Panting, Lindsey felt something else begin to swell from her belly, something different and yet very known. Suddenly, Ra bit her nipple, came down hard on it with her teeth, and the thick swelling inside Lindsey exploded. She gave one shout and leaned back further on the piling as her body accepted the orgasm, and there was nothing, nothing she could have done to stop or control it.

After a moment or an hour, she could feel Ra's arms around her, Ra standing in front of her. Still Lindsey leaned back on her hands, her breasts naked.

"I think I hear some people walking toward us," Ra said softly. "So I'm going to cover you up a little now, sweet woman."

Lindsey felt her T-shirt come down over her tender breasts, and Ra's hands helped her lean forward, then slide down into a standing position. Before her feet hit the ground, Lindsey wasn't sure her legs would take the weight, but they did. Ra pulled her shorts up for her and buttoned them. Then they stood quietly in an embrace as an invisible couple walked past the other side of their piling wall, involved in their own romance, Lindsey hoped.

"Want to walk back?"

Lindsey nodded, speechless.

They must have been in a time warp, Lindsey thought, as they ambled slowly toward town again, fingers entwined. The moon hadn't set yet, the crowds hadn't changed, and yet she and Ra had been out on the dock at least a lifetime. She felt groggy, heavy, as though she were climbing out of a long, deep sleep and hadn't quite reached awake.

Without speaking, they turned toward Mizmoon's. A pulse was pounding in the back of Lindsey's skull like a slow pronounced drumbeat, slightly off rhythm with her heartbeat. And her breast, the one Ra had bitten, felt bruised, leaving her more aware of her body, her sex, than usual.

Finally her brain began to focus again, and she realized she wanted to ask Ra some questions. She would probably never ask what she most wanted to know—What happened to me just then out on the pier?—even though she suspected Ra knew the answer.

"Tell me about Joan and Gabrielle," she suggested.

Ra nodded, understanding her indirect question, not surprised Lindsey knew their names. "We've all three been a family for six years now. Joan and I were lovers for seven years and then she met Gabrielle and fell in love with her, too. She and I were in a commuting relationship at that point. I was teaching in Boston, and she was taking a Jung seminar down in New York. That's where she met Gabrielle. I didn't want to lose Joan, so I had to find a way to learn to like the idea of Gabrielle."

Ra was telling the story very simply, with a hint of humor in her voice. Lindsey was sure she had told it a few times.

"How did you . . . are you and Gabrielle lovers?"

"Now we are. When Joan had a scare with breast cancer and was in the hospital for a biopsy, Gabrielle came up. She couldn't not be there. And we came to love more than the idea of one another." She was clearly amused now and looked at Lindsey for a response.

"It all sounds . . . so normal." Lindsey was at a loss for a better description. Somehow she had expected something more lurid from a ménage à trois.

"It is for us. Gabrielle moved her financial business up to Boston five years ago this summer. We lead busy lives. Joan and Gabrielle both travel in their work." She shrugged, ready to dismiss the subject.

"What's hard about it for you?" Lindsey wanted to know.

Ra thought for a moment. "When I was beginning to know Gabrielle, Joan was really angry and jealous. She thought we were taking advantage of her being in the hospital, that I was moving in on Gabrielle. But a lot of those feelings weren't about us. They were about her terror over the possibility of cancer. Now our hardest problem is finding time to be together." She smiled and squeezed Lindsey's hand tightly. "That's why we try and come out to the Cape most weekends. It gives us some time together. They'll be at the bar," she added as an afterthought. "I wanted you to meet them."

They arrived at the bar, and Ra led the way down the short winding stairs to the bar under a guesthouse. Lindsey could hear from the hum of conversation over the music that a larger-than-usual crowd had gathered tonight.

"Hey, Ra," Lisa's voice greeted them boisterously. "First time out this year?"

Then she saw Lindsey. "Oh, hi, Lindsey." She looked suspiciously from one to the other.

"Wow, Lisa, I really like your hair," Lindsey said quickly, hoping to distract her housemate from too much inquiry. Lisa's usually prominent afro had been cornrowed and beaded. "That's a gorgeous bead." She reached up to touch a delicate turquoise-and-white filigreed bead.

"Nigeria," Lisa said proudly. "Hand-painted. Some sisters from Trinidad gifted me with it. We spent the afternoon doing our hair thing." She laughed familiarly as she turned toward Ra. "So how you doing?"

Lindsey surveyed the bar as Lisa and Ra caught up. Her entire house was here tonight. Ellen hunched at a table in the corner with Michael and a skinny dark-haired faggot Lindsey didn't recognize. Must be the lead in *Torch Song*. Must be after midnight, too, she realized, if rehearsal was out. Up at the bar Angie was holding forth. The topic was AIDS, she could tell, and it seemed as though she and Joan, the therapist, were having a major disagreement. A few couples danced to an old "Men at Work" cut, and on the far side of the room

Lindsey could see that Danny and the sobriety crew had gathered by the coffee urn after the late-night AA meeting. Danny seemed to have a new diversion, a youngster, with an olive complexion and a mustache.

"We now have clear evidence of woman-to-woman transmission," Angie was insisting, as Lindsey and Ra wandered over to the far end of the bar. "Why do dykes think they're immune from what AIDS is doing to our community?"

"Because for all practical purposes, we are." Joan was slightly built but forceful. Dark hair, dark liner rimming her eyes, and a black silk shirt made her seem more powerful than Angie, even though Lindsey had seen Angie use her size to intimidate smaller women. Joan knew how to play the body language game. She leaned back on the bar, claiming space, telling Angie with her body that she was confident of her argument, her point of view.

"We're mostly affected because we're doing caretaking work again. Helping gay men learn how to have their feelings, cope with death, be responsible for one another for a change. We're holding their hands while they die, while they learn to grieve. We aren't dying. I only know one lesbian with AIDS, and she's a recovering I.V. drug user. Her lover of ten years is fine."

"Fine for now," Angie insisted. "This virus can be dormant for ten years. Why not protect ourselves? What's wrong with telling lesbians that *we* have to practice safe sex, too?"

Lindsey started to feel uncomfortably aware of Ra beside her, aware that Ra hadn't practiced anything resembling safe sex out there on the pier. Neither had she, she reminded herself. She'd let the risk be all Ra's.

Then Ra spoke. "There's nothing wrong with educating dykes, Angie. I think we need to be able to evaluate our own risks and then make choices we're comfortable with. There are two cases of woman-to-woman transmission right now, in 1990. The same year fifty-nine people were struck by lightning and died. I think we have to allow for some perspective, not just stop having sex or all rushing off to buy our dental dams." Ra spoke fairly gently, Lindsey thought, for someone who might be defending herself.

"It's just not possible to have perspective when the virus can hide for so long," Angie said angrily. "We may only have two cases today, but we don't know we *aren't* passing the virus continually among us. There's no way to be sure."

"That's true," Joan conceded. She looked ready to escape from the conversation, glad when Ra motioned her to one side, introduced her to Lindsey.

"Hi." Joan radiated enthusiasm. "You're the social worker Ra's been telling us about."

Lindsey laughed and groaned at the same time. "How could you do this to me?" she asked Ra. "What a fate. To be known as 'the social worker.' " Joan seemed nice, glad to meet her, not at all uptight or jealous or angry. Lindsey relaxed a little, leaning against the bar. And knew in that moment of relaxation how exhausted she was. She should say hello to a couple of people and then go crash. Ra and Joan were talking with two men Lindsey didn't know. She nodded to them all and wandered over to the corner of the bar where Danny sat.

When Lindsey finally unlocked her bike from behind Safe Harbor, instead of heading downtown toward the apartment, she turned the other direction up Route 6A. Soon she was pedaling hard past the edge of town and out along the bay road. Her bike light penetrated a narrow cone of visibility in the dark, now moonless, night. Her teeth were clenched, and anyone catching a glimpse of her face frowning in concentration would have said this woman was either very angry or on an urgent, emergency errand. Several miles out she took a sharp left away from the bay, jagged across the main highway, and cut into a road winding past Pilgrim Lake and into the dunes on the ocean side of the Cape.

She had biked out here a couple of times when she first arrived in order to jog on the path through the swamp, a wonderful two-mile run out to the ocean and then back into the dunes. She hadn't done it for a while. Mornings to sleep-in were too precious and then, well, she'd discovered the pleasures of having a couple of hours in the afternoon to lie on the beach at Herring Cove and watch the other dykes. But tonight she remembered the road as if she'd traveled it a thousand times and skidded to a halt in the deserted parking lot.

Lindsey needed to be alone with the sound of the ocean and the feel of the sand under her feet. Few people came here, even in daylight, because the beach was a half-mile walk down a sandy road. A few wide-wheeled vehicles with dune permits used this road as an access point to go up to the fishing beach near Race Point, but not many summer people bothered. Lindsey locked her bike and leaned it in the shadow of a dark hedge. She took the light out of its bracket and switched it on, checking to make sure she was on the right path, then turned it off again and waited for her eyes to adjust to the dark so she could walk toward the ocean. To her right, the lighthouse beam swept around every thirty seconds marking Head of the Meadow Beach. Soon she was able to discern the road and went forward. The mist reflected some of the light from Provincetown back down on this quiet dune. A few yards in, she bent and took off her sandals, then proceeded barefoot. The sand was deep in some places, hard in others, making walking difficult, but she was glad of the strain, glad to be making a physical effort. It slowed some of the questions racing through her mind enough for her to focus on one or two of them.

What had happened tonight? Why had she let Ra do that to her? No, why had she *asked* Ra to do that, for she had participated, she could not deny it. And why was she feeling this way now—ashamed, guilty, excited, and very unsure of a multitude of other feelings burbling away under the surface just beyond her conscious knowing.

"What about you?" she'd asked when Ra had come over to her at the bar later that night. "Don't you want. . ." She had flushed deeply with embarrassment, not knowing how to say it. "Shouldn't I come home with you? For a while anyway?"

Ra had smiled her half-amused, half-disbelieving smile. "Do *you* want to do that, Lindsey?"

No. Lindsey knew she didn't want to and didn't know how to say it, didn't know if she was supposed to say it. "I thought you might be feeling, well, left out." Then she blushed at how stupid that sounded.

"Ohhh." Ra looked like she understood more than Lindsey did. "You mean because I made love to you, I might be expecting reciprocity?" Her head tilted to one side as she watched Lindsey thoughtfully.

"That sounds so clinical," Lindsey said miserably, feeling tears catch at her throat.

"I'm sorry," Ra reached over and stroked Lindsey's cheek lightly. "Just know this, Lindsey. I *wanted* to have sex with you like that and don't feel left out at all. Quite the contrary, I was *very* satisfied. We don't all want the same thing from sex, you know, not each time anyway." She laughed, inviting Lindsey to share the joke with her, helping Lindsey out of her embarrassment. "I guess if you think about it, it's a good thing." Her voice softened, caressing Lindsey, "Believe me, you were wonderful."

Lindsey had noticed Ra's choice of words—*have sex with* instead of *make love*. She nodded, accepting Ra's comforting tone along with her description of what had happened between them.

"I guess I'll say good night, then. It's been a long day and a busy night." She blushed again. She meant at the restaurant, but didn't have the energy to explain.

Ra drew Lindsey into an embrace. "Good night to you, sweet woman. I'll look for you on the beach tomorrow. And if I miss you, we'll be back next weekend. Save our table on Friday night at Safe Harbor." She kissed Lindsey's forehead and cheeks and then released her.

Lindsey paused, not sure of anything, least of all whether she wanted to see Ra next weekend. But her need to seem O.K. overcame the fear, and she leaned forward to kiss Ra on the lips, all the assertion she could manage. "I'll look for you," she said, and turned toward the door.

The sandy road under her feet was harder now, easier walking, and her bare feet made no noise as she went forward. Lindsey could hear the surf breaking over the next rise of dunes and knew she had almost reached the beach. A short struggle upward, and then the dunes parted. Before her was the Atlantic Ocean, restless and powerful, beating in steady surf on the shore. She stood for a moment in the wind, letting the sound and feel of the ocean calm her racing heart. Here, at least, she was able to let go. Here, no one was watching. And if no one was expecting anything in particular of her, she could relax enough to see what it was she might be expecting of herself.

Not anxious to be down in the cool breeze coming off the water, Lindsey finally turned to her right and found a footpath leading out across the dune. She went just a short way from the road and then tucked herself down in the sand, sitting with her knees pulled up to her chin, staring out at the dark water, the lacy white froth of the waves racing diagonally across the beach. She sat there for a long time, the scene on the pier racing through her mind again and again, until what had happened no longer seemed strange, alien to her, until her responses seemed like something she, Lindsey Carter, might have experienced. She knew there would be more to learn from it. She would be able to talk with Sheila about it. Not now, but soon. She let the knowledge of some of the excitement and pleasure she had felt under the waning moonlight filter back into her body. The tension in her spine, along her jaw line, began to relax. Finally, she dozed.

She did not hear the soft purr of a dune wagon as it moved slowly, stealthily out onto the beach and turn up toward Race Point. She did not see two men come out of the buggy when it stopped and walk right to the water's edge as though they expected to see something out on the dark ocean. She was not awake to wonder how long they would stand there peering into darkness, nor to question why one of the men became impatient and shoved the other down in the sand. If she had seen, she might have thought they were lovers, one man lying back on the sand, his hands behind him, raising his head and chest slightly as the other leaned over him and grabbed his hair, pulling his head further back. She might have wondered if he made a lover's motion with his hand, moving back and forth, seeming to thrust at the man lying so open and vulnerable beneath him. But darkness would not have let her see much more, only that the man who had been standing straightened up after a while and walked back to the dune buggy. As he got in on the passenger side, the vehicle began to pull away, going on up the beach, leaving the other man lying in the sand, a dark shadow among the seaweed. The lighthouse beam rotated slowly, flashing its warning into the darkness.

Just before dawn, Lindsey woke shivering, stretched, climbed down the dune to the road, and walked rapidly toward her bike in the growing daylight.

Chapter Four

I believe in magic. Do you? I believe in both kinds. There's the easy stuff like coincidences. Like I want to talk to someone and, as I'm thinking about calling them, the phone rings and guess who? Or like when you're feeling all dewy-eyed about somebody and the sky gives you a double rainbow. That's the easy stuff.

But I believe in the other kind of magic too. The kind that's just one step beyond *only justice can stop a curse*. The kind of magic that can pull different forms of power into alignment and make things happen that we have no explanation for in our rational minds. Spontaneous remissions of cancer. UFOs. Voices of spirits speaking through mediums to our world. That sort of thing. I never believed in Santa Claus, of course. He seemed too unlikely to my four- or five-year-old mind. But a potion that can bring a wandering lover back home? A chant to cure malaria? Well, why not? People have survived torture and lived to walk among us as normal human beings, people who can love and laugh and want to live. What's so hard to believe about magic? That idea of an omnipotent God who dispenses justice is a lot harder to imagine. To my mind, that's about as unlikely as Santa Claus.

I was thinking about these things because when I finally dragged myself out of bed on Sunday at noon or so, the first thing Angie told me was that there had been a murder out at High Head Beach. My whole system went into shock. I got cold, and my heart slowed down and started to beat very loudly. No one at the house knew where I'd been most of the night. In fact, I was sure they thought I'd gone to

Ra's. When I came back to the house at sunrise, everyone was asleep. I crawled into bed too, hoping for a few hours of brain death.

Then Angie told me the rest of it. She collects news the way a vacuum cleaner picks up dust. None of this had hit the newspapers yet, you understand, but Angie had gone into the Little Store for the Sunday *Boston Globe* and Richard had just talked to Sal who'd come from the early morning AA meeting at City Hall which also houses the Police Department where Sal had talked to a buddy of his who was a dispatcher who told him about the murder.

The beach patrol had been rounding up kids who sneak out to sleep on the beach, taking the dune buggy the length of the beach from Head of the Meadow to Race Point, when they came upon the body. It was just above the tideline. The dispatcher didn't have many details about tire marks and footprints, but it looked like a hate crime. He'd been wearing a shirt and shorts. The shirt was open, and somebody had carved the word *FAG* on his chest with the same knife that had been used to slit his throat. And his shorts were down around his knees, leaving him exposed. No one was saying whether he'd been sexually mutilated or tortured. Since the footprints had probably been washed away by the tide, Angie and Richard agreed it was doubtful the police could know how many had taken part in this murder.

So I was freaking out that the murder had probably occurred while I was meditating on life's vagaries up there on the dune. And I was freaking out about the details—I knew what it felt like to have your shorts pulled down, your chest exposed. I didn't want to hide the fact I'd been at the beach last night, but I wasn't going to let anybody know about the second part of it. I tried not to think about synchronicity, or those two things happening on opposite sides of this narrow spit of sand we call Cape Cod, happening with such different results. But I was definitely taking it personally. You might say I felt it as a personal offense, a personal violation.

Naturally, as soon as I told Angie where I'd been most of the night, she made me call the dispatcher at the police station. I told them I'd been up there, that the recent footprints in the dunes were mine, and that I hadn't seen anything at all. But Sal's friend Eddie said they'd be sending somebody over to take a statement from me, since it might help establish the time element.

The questions I got asked eventually by the P-town P.D. were nothing compared to the grilling from Angie as soon as I hung up.

"What were you doing out there in the middle of the night?"

"Thinking."

"I don't buy it. You're not that stupid. Tell me the truth. You weren't really alone, you just don't want us to know who you were with."

"Get off it, Angie. I needed some time to think. Where do I ever get any privacy? We're crowded in these four rooms like it was a roach hotel."

"You could *think* out there in the middle of the day. If you'd been thinking last night, you'd have known how dangerous it was. Those sailors who come for the fleet blessing, I've told you what kinds of things have happened here other years. What's wrong with your head, girl?"

Angie's face was getting pink with indignation as she imagined all the things that could have happened to me, I guess. I still wasn't sure why Angie was getting so upset about my safety—in general, I mean—but it was starting to make me uncomfortable. Angry, actually, is what it was making me.

Lisa was listening by now, leaning against the frame of the door to her and Ellen's room.

"Leave the woman alone, Angie. You think you're the only one in this house allowed to take risks."

"What does *that* mean?" Angie swung around to face Lisa, who shrugged.

"If the shoe fits, sweetie."

"I evaluate the risks I am taking," Angie insisted.

"Maybe Lindsey does too." She turned back into the bedroom to cut off the conversation.

And what was that about? I'd never seen Lisa challenge anyone before, even this mildly. Mostly she was laid back and occasionally she was sarcastic. Sarcasm was a useful tool, I knew, when you didn't want to engage, just snipe. Lisa had left herself open when she challenged Angie like that. Unless, of course, she knew that Angie wouldn't call her on it. Too complex for me, I decided, and let it go. But I couldn't help but wonder what risks Angie was taking and whether there was some other reason she was so concerned about me.

We were all awake for the interview with the police sergeant when he finally showed, but it was distinctly anticlimactic. He didn't ask why I was there at all, just what time, did I come in a vehicle, when did I leave, and did I see anything that might be helpful? Angie tried to grill him about the details, but he just said there was nothing he could reveal at this time, nodded politely, and left.

"I'm for the beach," Ellen announced between yawns. "Enough of this excitement. I want a few calming rays and the smell of suntan lotion on warm female skin before I have to deal with the boys in rehearsal this afternoon."

Ellen was coming back in enough time for me to get to work, so I left my bike locked up and hitched a ride over to Herring Cove with her.

We'd no sooner found our spot and stretched out among the crowd when Danny came loping over and plopped himself down in the sand next to us. Ellen groaned and turned her face into the blanket.

"Hi, Lindsey. Hi, Ellen. Ellen," he didn't pause for breath or responses, "I've been meaning to ask you. Do you have any openings at the theater—parts, understudies, ushers, that sort of thing?"

"No, Danny." Her voice was muffled by the blanket, and she didn't turn over to look at him.

"Oh, I was hoping. . .there's this really neat guy I've met. Very talented, I think. You'd like him. Jose Alfredo. He's Latino," Danny added, rather unnecessarily, I thought.

"Danny, it's a Jewish play, and all of our jobs have been filled for weeks."

"I *know* the play rather well," Danny huffed. "There are other parts in it, Ellen. Have you got an understudy for Alan yet?"

Ellen groaned again. I knew she was imagining a character named Alan with a Spanish accent.

"Come on, Danny," I intervened. "I'd like to meet him. Where are you guys stationed?"

We walked over to Danny's blanket, picking our way through the half-naked bodies and beach debris. Herring Cove isn't the most lovely of P-town's beaches, but it certainly has the most casual dress code—when the Park rangers aren't around.

Dykes and fags who come to the beach seem to fall at either end of a wide spectrum. It's luxury or spartan. I seldom see anything in between. And I can't say fags do one thing and dykes another. It's genderless, this phenomenon. Danny, of course, was a spartan. I say of course because he lived that way all summer, owning only a couple items of clothing, trading and borrowing when he wanted variety. He'd give away his next-to-last shirt if someone admired it. I think he was comfortable living like that for now, since he knew he was going to be a very rich Harvard M.B.A. someday soon. Possessions are a responsibility, and Danny was putting off responsibility as long as he could.

Next to Danny and Jose's two small well-worn towels were four faggots who'd brought their entire motel room out on the beach. Several blankets to claim space, a stereo box, a cooler with ice, eight different levels of sunscreen—the bottles lined up in a neat row—a volleyball, frisbee, and kite, and an umbrella. We may have watched this crew, or a similar bunch, trudge through the sand on their way to the perfect spot. One ingenious couple had slung the cooler, a basket, four lawn chairs, and two plastic bags on a pole they carried over their shoulders, all the stuff strung out between them. The dykes in my area were envious anybody had that much forethought about going to the beach. I imagined those guys had been planning their entrance all winter. I crouched on the edge of a frayed towel and could only hope Danny and Jose's neighbors wouldn't let them die of dehydration before they offered them a soda.

Jose Alfredo was the young man I'd seen Danny with last night. Close in, he didn't look quite so juvenile. Behind the smooth skin and baby-soft black hair and mustache were eyes that had seen some sad or tragic things, I thought. He said what country he was from down there, but it might have been any of them. I could never distinguish Uruguay from Ecuador from Paraguay. He didn't say he was from Colombia, I'm sure of that, since we all know their only export these days is cocaine and, along with Panama and Nicaragua, they've gotten themselves on the official U.S. hate list.

Then Jose Alfredo went down to the water for a swim, and Danny asked me what was wrong.

"Did you hear about last night's murder?"

"Yeah. Why has it got you so upset? I mean, it's awful. And it looks like fag bashing carried to the extreme. But I would have thought it would make you angry, maybe, not depressed."

Like I said, Danny reads me pretty well. I told him half of it. Not about the pier with Ra, but that I'd been out on the dunes, probably not far above where it happened, and how that was freaking me out.

"Wow." Danny was impressed. "And you didn't see anything? You can't remember anything that would catch these creeps?"

"Nothing," I admitted, made more miserable by the sudden realization that if I'd stayed awake and pondered the nature of existence like I'd meant to, I might have been able to solve this hate crime right away.

"It must have been fairly quiet," Danny realized. "Or you'd have woken up. If there'd been a whole bunch of drunk guys shouting, you probably would have noticed."

"That's true, Danny. It was a quiet night, not much wind, and the surf was low. No real loud wave noise. Do you think the cops have thought of that yet?"

"Who knows if they'll ever think of anything," Danny said glumly. "Let's don't mention it in front of Jose," he asked, as the young man walked slowly back toward us. "He heard the victim was Latino, and I think he's real upset. Waiting for a police I.D. He might even have known him."

I didn't say anything else then. I was impressed that Danny knew something Angie had not been able to grill out of her sources. I wanted to ask him how he knew this, or how Jose found it out, but that would have to wait for the restaurant tonight, I decided.

I was heading back to my towel and a quiet nap when Lisa hailed me from up in the dunes. I waved and paused. She was with the three dykes from Trinidad, and I wasn't sure I had any energy for new people.

On the other hand, I thought as I trudged up the dune to their pocket in the sun, from what Lisa said they sounded like the most interesting trio to hit town this summer.

"Hi, Lisa. Too cool for you in the breeze down there on the beach?" I wiped my brow in mock dismay.

"You white people don't really like the sun, do you?" Lisa tossed back at me. "Why do you spend so much time trying to look like you were born in it?"

"Just envy, I guess, Lisa." I was only half joking as I tried not to feel inferior and pale and uninteresting sitting next to the four of them. Even Lisa's chocolate brown skin looked light to me when she was so close to women who were really black. I found the hue and tone of their skin color incredible. All three of these women seemed to radiate the warmth that is the essence of black—that is, the sum of all colors. In one light, I could catch a cast of blue, in another a slight red tone. All in all, I was quite taken and would have sat happily staring all afternoon. But Lisa was doing introductions.

"Lindsey, meet Gloria, Sindar, and Evelyn." We nodded. "They're a vocal and drumming trio, here to open at The Loft next week."

"That's fantastic!" Not only was I enthusiastic, I was laughing at Lisa's managing to keep this fact from Angie for a whole day. Information control was Lisa's way of fighting with Angie, I'd begun to realize, and nothing made Angie more furious. It was a long-standing feud, one they'd started before I came on the scene. I turned to Gloria, who seemed the oldest of the three, to ask where they'd been playing before P-town, when Lisa interrupted.

"I told them you were out on the dunes last night—right there where the murder happened."

"Oh." I felt deflated. It wasn't me Lisa had been calling over, it was my closeness to this murder. In Evanston, we had a next-door neighbor whose teenage son was forever in trouble, usually more bizarre than serious trouble. She used to say, "Well, I could dine out for a week on Mickey's latest exploit." She meant that people were interested in what had happened and would invite her to dinner to hear about it. It had always seemed a weird concept to me, but it was beginning to occur to me that I could dine out for quite a while on being so close to a murder, even if I hadn't noticed a thing.

"You must be a special person." It was the short, round woman named Sindar speaking in a gently rolling voice. "To be able to walk on the dunes in the dark is a gift. Were you afraid?"

"I was afraid," I admitted, "but not of the dunes." I said the words before I thought them, partly in response to the friendliness of her inquiry. But then she waited, as if I were able to explain what I meant by that, as if I even understood what I meant.

"I was upset," I equivocated. Then, "Yeah, I guess I was scared. Scared of too many people and all the confusion in town." That was a slight evasion. The confusion hadn't been in town, it was in me. "So I biked out to the dunes where I could be alone. I'm never afraid of nature. Just respectful." She was nodding as though she understood what I was saying.

Then I remembered what Danny had told me. "There's a rumor that the victim was Latino," I said to Lisa.

"Of course," Lisa said bitterly. "A person of color. What else is new? Were there any rope marks on his neck? Shit. Sometimes I get so tired." She turned her palms up in a momentary gesture of defeat.

I didn't know what to say. I hadn't automatically made that identification the way Lisa had—person of color. That made him one of hers, in a sense, not as closely as he was one of Jose Alfredo's people, but close enough to have reminded Lisa of her vulnerability.

"That is bad, very bad," said Gloria, and her two friends were nodding, so I nodded too.

"Yes," Sindar agreed. "It gives a permission, it sets an atmosphere. Especially if they do not find out right away who did this thing."

"Yeah," Lisa added glumly. "And you can bet we won't see the white gay men getting very excited about this, not like if he'd been one of *them.*

I wanted to disagree with her. I wished I could disagree with her. But I knew she was more right than wrong. I sat with them for a few more minutes, then left, feeling more depressed than I had in a long, long time.

I was still trying to wend my way back to my towel and my nap when I tripped over Ra and Gabrielle. I stopped for a minute when Ra reminded me that I hadn't been introduced to Gabrielle last night. Now this fascinated me. I had seen Gabrielle Friday night at Safe Harbor, but I'd been so preoccupied with the cleavage peaking out at me from Ra's blouse, I hadn't really focused on her. If Ra was sexy, and Joan powerful, Gabrielle. . .well, frankly, she looked like a housewife from Evanston. Not the modern swinging kind, either, but somebody about my mother's age who didn't care so much about her figure, probably cut her hair herself, used lipstick when she really wanted to look dressed up. I'm talking plain. With a name like Gabrielle, I thought she'd at least have a French accent, but her roots were more Canadian than French, and more northern Maine than Canadian. You know what, though? I'd trust this face with my money. If I had any, I mean. She seemed totally honest and open, and she seemed to like me right away. I guessed this was going to be a summer for preconceptions to bite the dust. I couldn't wait to tell Sheila about meeting this ménage à trois.

They'd heard about the murder, of course. I didn't tell them I was playing a starring role, since I would rather not tell Ra where I'd gone after I left the bar last night. But I did say I'd heard the victim was Latino.

"That's interesting," Ra mused. "There aren't too many Hispanics around here other than the Portuguese. Are you sure he wasn't Portuguese?"

I said I didn't have a clue who or what he was.

"If he was Portuguese, he would have been a local and the police could have gotten an I.D. on him right away," Joan said practically. "If he was Latino and not from around here and there was no I.D. on him, it may take years for them to figure out who he was."

"It's true," Ra agreed. "There are a lot of undocumented people from Latin America living in and around Boston right now. If he was illegal, they may never know his name." Then she added, "I wonder if it was drug related?"

"Danny says P-town is a place where people come to be anonymous," I remembered suddenly. "He doesn't have to be illegal. It could have been any one of us who is out here escaping our past life. Danny says P-town is like one big AA meeting, only it's anonymity without the sobriety."

Suddenly we all began to laugh at the concept.

"Hi, my name's Ra," Ra said, "and I'm hiding from my ex-lover."

"Right. My name's Lindsey, and I'm pretending to be a wealthy dyke on vacation."

"Well, you've got a pretty good disguise then," Gabrielle drawled at me, "working at Safe Harbor."

"Oh, yeah. Right. So much for pretenses." I was starting to feel a little awkward as we played this game and realized I still didn't know Ra's last name.

"We all have hidden pasts," Ra said, shrugging as though it didn't matter. "There's not a person on this beach who doesn't have something that's defined as a secret, something they're ashamed of—or afraid of. Isn't that right, Lindsey?

She smiled at me when she asked the question, a kind smile, but I got the sense again that I amused her and I wasn't sure why.

"Say, Lindsey," Gabrielle changed the subject. "Angie told us you're working at the Feminist Writer's Conference next week."

I nodded. I was. I'd foolishly agreed to give up my two days off on Tuesday and Wednesday and my beach time on Thursday and Friday for this event. I'd applied for the job the first day I got here when I wasn't sure I'd be able to earn enough to survive and still take something home toward my living expenses for the second year of grad school.

"A couple of friends of mine are coming out to teach at it," Gabrielle said, and named the most famous lesbian poet in the country and a very well-known bisexual Black fiction writer. Why was I surprised? This housewife's exterior hid some very fascinating things. Gabrielle would never need anonymity. She had cultivated the ultimate in a plain brown wrapper.

"It should be interesting. They told me I could have a pass for some of the evening readings, but I'll be working nights at the restaurant. I'm going to sit in on a couple of the afternoon workshop sessions instead."

"Do you write?" Gabrielle asked me.

"No," I admitted, "but I read a lot. We were assigned some of these writers in Women's Studies classes when I was in college, so I didn't think I should pass up a chance like this to hear them firsthand."

I paused. Gabrielle's face just invited secrets, let me tell you. "Actually, I do write some. Mostly journal-type stuff. And not for publication," I hastened to add, "just for my own record. I like to remember what I've been thinking about from day to day."

Gabrielle didn't seem surprised, nor did she push me for more information than I was willing to give. "It should be interesting for you, then," was all she said. And I refrained from rushing to confess that I'd had a crush on the famous fiction writer since I'd seen her picture in *Ms.* magazine ten years ago when I was sixteen, horny, and very impressionable. As my eyes kept sliding back to Ra, who was sunbathing without her bathing suit top on, I wondered if I was so different at twenty-six. I certainly still felt horny and impressionable. More of the first and less of the latter, I hoped.

Gabrielle didn't do anything stupid, like tell me to say hello to her friends for her or things like that. And she hadn't used just their first names when she was saying she knew them. I hate that. Like everybody should know who you mean when you say, *Oh, I saw Rita the other day*, like you'd forgotten not everybody knew Rita Mae Brown to say hello to. I had the feeling Gabrielle wasn't name dropping.

When I finally got back to my towel, Angie was there, having a heated discussion with Ellen, so I turned away and headed down to the water. It was time for my daily immersion and past time for my nap. I could tell I was not going to be Ms. Sweetness and Light at work tonight.

I sat on the edge of the surf after I swam and focused my eyes straight ahead on the surf sliding in, breaking, falling back. The rhythm and noise of it were calming and made the whole world behind me fade away. It was almost like being alone.

As I settled, and the world sank in the sand behind me, I began to feel the sadness that I carried away from talking with Lisa and her friends. Five years had passed since Belle walked away from me, but I still felt something was unfinished with her, some connection between us that had never been severed. Ra was right: I did have a secret. But I wasn't sure why I would call it a secret. I wasn't afraid to tell people about Belle, and certainly I wasn't ashamed. It was more that I felt protective of—what? Not Belle. Maybe of the naive eighteen-year-old I had been, the one who held her dreams right out there in the light for anyone to see.

I'd thought racism had been fixed when I went off to college. Certainly that was how it was talked about in my home. Schools were integrated, everyone had equal opportunities, and we white people had an obligation to treat Black people with respect. I hadn't noticed the other lessons, the ones that weren't verbal. My parents had no friends who were Black, Latino, Asian, or Native American. Our affluent white suburb was surrounded by neighborhoods where people weren't making it, weren't even getting by. And all the people who lived in those neighborhoods had darker skin than mine. When I found out Belle was going to be my freshman roommate, my parents were pleased. Racism may have been gone, but they were sure I would act better to Belle than some of the other students. I tried.

When I'd been talking to Lisa earlier, I thought about doing something to protest the murder out on the dunes, to say to the world it isn't O.K. to hate like that. Carving FAG on somebody's chest is not O.K. Then Lisa reminded me the victim was a person of color and I got scared. I could feel myself backing away from doing something. Sitting here staring at the waves, I wasn't sure what I was afraid of, but the fear still held me back, just like someone was standing in front of me, pressing my shoulders to a wall.

The tide was coming in, and the waves were not just tickling my toes any more, they were starting to break very close to where I was hunched and spread out up the shore behind me. I was wishing Sheila were here, wishing I had someone I trusted to test these feelings on.

"Are you planning on moving? Or were you going to sit there until a wave carries you back up to the beach? I don't mean to bother you," the voice behind me said, "but I was starting to worry about you a little."

The voice sounded familiar, but it wasn't someone I recognized. A good thing, too, because I didn't want to talk to anyone I knew in P-town just then. I turned around, torn between curious and resentful, and found myself looking up the length of a gorgeous, lithe body and into those deep-green eyes.

Let me drown, I thought deliriously, but only in those sea-green eyes. Let me live, but only if I'm not dreaming.

Chapter Five

It had been a summer for those goofy Harlequin romances. Angie started it, of course, when we ran out of lesbian romances to read and pass around the house, then on to the next group. Angie was pissed that "our" presses couldn't seem to keep up with the demand. There were only a few dozen new romances a year, and once you'd read all the reprints of the dyke novels from the forties and fifties, well, what was a girl to do? Read Harlequins and change the pronouns was Angie's solution. So along to the beach came the funky little paperbacks. At least they were lightweight in a couple of ways. They didn't put a strain on your brain, and it was possible to hold them over your head and read while lying on your back. *War and Peace* was never meant for beach reading.

I don't think I ever read one all the way through, but when Angie got to a juicy part (once or twice, max, in a novel), she'd roll over, say, "Hey, listen to this," and commence to give us a dramatic rendition, complete with changed pronouns so we wouldn't be offended, or politically grossed out, or whatever.

It wasn't always easy to tell when things were about to get hot and heavy, though, because in these stories the lovers would pant at one another from a respectful distance, like across a table, several times before "doing it." "Listen," Angie would demand, changing pronouns and masculine gender names as she read.

" 'There was a faintly challenging light in those distinctive eyes now, one that Helen wasn't sure she was ready to meet. She was drawn to this (woman) like a needle to a magnet, intoxicated by the potent force of (her) glorious (femininity). Sitting opposite (her) like this, it was impossible not to let her eyes dwell on the firm, lithe body, the broad shoulders and tapering waist and hips, the glorious mane of (her) hair. Just looking, she felt her pulse begin to quicken in response to the pull of (her) attraction—but whether she was prepared to take things any further was a different matter, one she hadn't yet decided in her own mind.' "

"Oh, goddess, I can't stand it," Ellen or Lisa or I would groan. "Why don't they get on with it?"

Ellen was quite sure switching the pronouns created an inaccurate picture of lesbian lust, since she'd never met two dykes who waited 153 pages to do it in her life. Lisa said it probably was a fairly inaccurate picture of heterosexuals, too, but Angie was undeterred and read on.

" 'And now there was no time for words or thoughts, only for reaction and sensation, the vibrant awareness of total concentration on another person that drove away all doubts, all other feeling from her mind as she abandoned herself to (Colleen's) embrace, drowning in sensual awareness, overwhelmed by burning desire and the aching longing to communicate that feeling to. . .' "

"Have they done it yet, Angie? I mean, I can't tell from what you're reading there." Lisa always liked to know the basics.

"It's the foreplay, Lisa," Ellen countered. "You have to have a sense of drama to understand this."

"Why don't they use real words?" I wanted to know. "I mean, you never can tell if any of their parts are touching or what position they're in. What use is it?"

"I didn't know you were doing a research project, Lindsey," Angie chided me. And I blushed, of course, and shut up.

"I think one starts undoing the other's buttons in a few more pages," Angie ventured. "You sort of have to hang in there."

"Not me," Lisa said, pushing to her feet. "Sorry, girls, but I've got a life to live. You know, REAL life?"

Actually, I kind of liked the romances. They were all written according to the same formula. Unlike real life, you could always tell the good people from the bad people, and nothing bad ever happened to good people. Sometimes it would seem like it was about to happen to them, but an amazing series of circumstances and coincidences would intervene. Angie had one of the romance/intrigue genre where the heroine and her boyfriend were shot at seven times, tied up in a burning barn once, had knives thrown at them three times, were attacked by a fast-moving vehicle twice, were locked in an abandoned house with three armed men determined to kill them—and they were never hurt, not even bruised. How can James Bond compete with that? Face it, most people's lives can't compete with these books for happy endings. Conflict and misunderstandings never last more than five pages, hidden secrets in people's pasts can explain 95 percent of the evil in the world. It's only a matter of sticking it out until you get to the happy ending.

So I sat there as the waves washed around me and stared up at the woman who'd ask me if I wanted to drown. She was Wholesome, Carol, the Nun from the restaurant the night before, and her white tank suit didn't hide a thing. Not the thrust of her nipples hardening from the chilly spray of the waves, not the curling little honey-blonde hairs peaking out of her crotch line, nor the pout of her lower lip as she stood with her hands on her trim hips staring at me, waiting for me to say something. Or, at the very least, for me to be tipped over by a wave and sent tumbling into shore.

Then she smiled and reached a hand out to me. What could I do but reach up to her grasp and let myself be pulled to my feet?

But this was real life, not a romance novel. Naturally I couldn't think of anything to say that made sense.

"Thanks." Then, of course, I blushed.

"I wasn't sure you wanted to be rescued," her green eyes were laughing a little, but she seemed shy, too. That made me relax a bit.

I shrugged. "Sometimes I think so hard, it's like I'm on another planet." And we were both silent, staring at one another. Where was the next chapter in the *Cruising Manual* when you needed it?

"My name's—"

"I'm Lindsey—" We'd both blurted it out at the same time and then stopped to blush again.

"I. . .you. . .I met you at the restaurant last night," she said finally. "My name's Carol."

"Sure. I remember. Hi, Carol. I'm Lindsey."

We started to wander along the surf's edge without either of us suggesting it, our bodies moving in an easy rhythm.

"What were you thinking about, Lindsey?" She sounded like she really wanted to know, and I had been longing for someone to tell. So in a few minutes, improbable as it was for me to be doing, I was pouring it all out to her—the murder, being up on the dunes, talking to the police, wishing I'd been awake and seen something that would catch the murderers, hearing from Danny that the victim was maybe Latino, *a person of color* in Lisa's words.

She listened the way I always wanted to be listened to, with total attention and without her own visible agenda. Sheila listens to me, but she always has some advice, some opinion on what I ought to be doing or thinking or saying, and she can't wait for me to get to the end of what I'm saying before she's there with her stuff. She calls it interaction and values that way of communicating very highly. I accuse her of making conversation a competitive sport, too, just like our grad classes. But I need her too much to complain too much. Especially when most people don't really listen at all. Check it out sometime. Maybe they'll hear a third of what you're saying, maybe a half. I do it myself. It can be hard to turn myself off long enough to be receptive, to just be quiet and listen.

Carol was receptive. I could see she was troubled by some of what I was telling her, but she waited until I was finished. Or at least until I paused.

"Do you think she's right? The woman who said this will act as a kind of permission for other acts of violence against gay people?"

We had walked pretty far out toward the point now, away from the more crowded beach, past the dyke area, beyond the stretch the faggots had claimed. She paused when I paused and may have had the same thought, since we both turned to walk back the other way— that this wasn't the best setting to be discussing murder in the dunes and hate crimes against lesbians and gays.

"I hope she's not right," I answered her finally, "but I'm afraid she is. I don't like what it might mean for gay people and Provincetown."

She nodded. "I think I know what you mean. This is an extraordinary place. I'd never been here before this week. My friends said it was a place gay people went, but I couldn't imagine what they meant by that until I'd seen this." She waved her hand toward the gay men, clustered in two's, three's, and four's on their blankets and towels. A couple in the near foreground were sleeping, one man's head resting on his lover's belly. Next to them, a sun-darkened adonis was rubbing suntan lotion into his lover's buttocks with passionate attention to detail. A volleyball game stretched across the sand, and in the two minutes we'd paused to watch, I'd seen more body-to-body contact than in a year of professional football.

What did Carol make of it all? A thousand questions raced through my head, a million things I wanted to know about her instantly. If I'd been Ra, I chided myself, I would have come on to her by now, never would have turned away from the deserted end of the beach until...until what? I couldn't imagine it. For now, this was enough, walking in the sun along the surf's edge, occasionally bumping hips or shoulders.

And then in the sunlight I saw the white band around her sun-tanned ring finger. I took her hand in mine and raised it, looking obviously at the blank space where her ring had been last night. My eyes asked the question I couldn't seem to voice.

She sighed, sensing it was her turn now.

"Look, it's too much to explain all at once. I don't even understand it myself."

"O.K. Does that mean I can see you again? I have to go to work pretty soon." We were walking past the dykes in the sand now, and I refrained from looking for Ellen amidst the bodies. I wasn't ready to let Carol go yet.

"Maybe I can stop into the restaurant again tonight," Carol offered.

I nodded, but it wasn't enough. "Where are you staying?"

"We're at Maggie's—it's a bed and breakfast. Some friends of friends run it. Do you know Brenda and Cory?"

"No, but I know the place." Two more things I needed. "How long are you staying?"

"Forever," Carol blurted out, then laughed a little crazily, I thought, and then she started to cry.

"That's O.K. with me," I put my arm around her shoulders, not sure what to say. It seemed like a hug was what she needed. Never mind how warm and smooth her thighs touching my thighs are.

Ignore the scent of her hair tickling my nose. Pretend I don't notice the wetness starting in my cunt. This is just a hug, a friendly hug.

"Linnnndsey." It was Ellen, screeching from up by the parking lot. Goddess, not now.

I turned and waved to let her know I was coming. "My ride is leaving," I explained to Carol, hating to leave her, not wanting to move my body one inch away from her soft warm skin. In the romance novels, it would not have happened like this, I can assure you.

"It's O.K. I'm O.K. Oh, I'm sorry," Carol sniffled, as she tried to smile. "I didn't mean to be so stupid."

I touched her cheek with my hand and brushed my lips along her forehead, tasting salt and sun. "I really want to see you tonight," I whispered in her ear. "Promise me you'll come by this evening. There's so much I want to talk with you about," I ended lamely.

She nodded. Her eyes looked solemnly into mine. Honest, they *were* sea-green, the centers lighter than the edges, which gave them such power, even now when she'd been crying.

"Linnndsey. I'm gooooooing."

I waved as I turned and ran toward the parking lot, my feet winging across the burning sand, lifting me into joy. And I didn't know her last name.

"WHO was that woman you were making out with?" Ellen wanted to know as soon as I got to the car. What a jolt. Reality. She was looking at me like I was auditioning for a part.

"Ummm. Just somebody I met. Around town." Then as an afterthought I added, "I wasn't making out with her, Ellen. She was upset and needed a hug." Not that I had felt like her sister or her aunt or anything when I'd been giving her that hug.

"Right." Ellen was still examining me out of the corner of her eye as she drove through late afternoon pedestrians swarming around the P-town monument. "So what's her name and what does she do and where is she from and all that?"

"Ummm. Her name is Carol." That was it, about all the information I had, at least all I was willing to share with Ellen. So I changed the subject, quick.

"Ellen, I think we need to plan something, something like a memorial service—but not exactly—for the guy who was murdered.

Even if we don't know who he is. I mean, who he was. Don't you think we need to do something to say we noticed he had the word *FAG* carved on his chest?" Before she could answer, I rushed to add the clincher. "If there's any, you know, ceremony, you'd be the one to plan it, make sure it went right and all."

Ellen was looking at me with a different kind of interest now. "Yeah, maybe. Let's wait until tomorrow and see what the papers say, see if the police have identified him and stuff. If he has a family, if they're local people, they might not be wild about having a bunch of queers claiming him. Not that we couldn't," she rushed to add.

I nodded. "Right. It would be good if we could get more information. Keep your ears open at rehearsal tonight. Maybe check with a couple of the guys and see what they think, O.K?"

I rushed through my shower, visions of green eyes and the promise of tonight propelling me eagerly toward Safe Harbor. Had it been only a few short hours ago I'd been dreading this evening? I hoped this adrenalin surge would carry me through at least part of it. My body ached from its various exercises of the day before, and I felt right on the edge of exhaustion after my night on the dunes. And now, Carol. A woman out of my dream life. Maybe it wasn't exhaustion I was on the edge of. Try hysteria. Or panic.

Normally able to select her own clothes, Lindsey fiddled precious minutes away staring into her closet. She selected one blouse, tried it on in front of the mirror, gave a disgusted shrug, and took it off again. Nothing pleased her, but her watch alarm beep-beeped at her and she knew the next thing she put on her body was what she would see Carol in tonight. Quickly she grabbed a clean pair of white cutoffs from her drawer and pulled a blue-green cotton shirt over her head. She wanted to see the color reflected back at her in Carol's eyes.

By nine o'clock Lindsey had worked five hours and was beginning to move from panic to depression. Carol hadn't come into the restaurant. What if she didn't? Could Lindsey actually walk over to Maggie's and knock on the door? She spent the first half of the evening worrying about whether Carol would come in alone or with her two friends. The second half she fought a growing depression as she became convinced that Carol had changed her mind, had gone back to her friends, checked out of the guesthouse, and was now fleeing to whatever part of the world she had appeared from.

And Carol? Lindsey couldn't imagine that this poised, gorgeous, apparently self-assured woman would have a moment of self-doubt or hesitation. How could she have known that, as Lindsey bounded toward the parking lot, Carol stood on the beach asking herself if she was crazy, crazy to confide in this stranger?

Lindsey was learning about masks, and she was beginning to see past the mask if someone like Danny dropped their facade for a moment. But she hadn't yet learned how fear can create a shell of apparent calmness. As the evening dragged on, her only thought was that Carol had changed her mind, found something more interesting to do with someone more interesting than Lindsey. She grew increasingly depressed as she convinced herself that this was true.

Lindsey would never have thought that by nine o'clock Carol had paced the length of Commercial Street three times. Having told Andrea and Maureen she was having dinner with a woman she met on the beach, ignored the look that passed between them, and fled downtown alone, she was afraid to go home and afraid to go into the restaurant.

Now Carol stood on the sidewalk across the street from Safe Harbor, apparently fascinated by the large, green Teenage Mutant Ninja Turtle figures silkscreened on T-shirts in the window.

It was Danny who finally spotted her. He was hanging out on the sidewalk outside the restaurant during a slow period, his arm slung casually over Jose Alfredo's shoulder. He knew who Carol was right away—the nun from last night. And it didn't take much for him to guess who she was waiting to see. He paused for a minute, wondering if she knew Lindsey didn't get finished until eleven. Even a nun couldn't stare into that window for another two hours, he decided, and went inside to tell Lindsey her friend was waiting for her across the street. For his reward, he got to watch Lindsey's face go from grim to ecstatic in an instant.

"Where? Oh, wow. Danny, thank you." She left the tray she'd been stacking dirty dishes on and dashed out of the restaurant. Carol was gone, she thought in a panic. And then she saw her in front of the drugstore, staring disconsolately at a sunglasses display.

"You can come into the restaurant, you know," Lindsey said shyly, standing beside and a little behind Carol. "The manager won't mind if you don't want to eat dinner."

Carol spun around to face Lindsey when she first spoke and stared at her, seeming not to comprehend. Her face relaxed into a smile, then into a large, relieved grin.

Lindsey saw Carol's acquiescence, but not her relief. It was enough. She led Carol into Safe Harbor and sat her at a small table in a corner. A thousand questions raced through Lindsey's mind. Why were you waiting out there? Why didn't you come in? Didn't you know how worried I'd be? But "what kind of dressing do you want on your salad?" was the only question she could ask. She watched Carol nibbling her salad, watching Lindsey work, and when she finally got a break, she slid into the empty chair opposite Carol. They sat, smiling at one another, as though they had achieved something quite marvelous through great effort.

By closing time they'd gotten through the "I'm from. . ." and "I work at. . ." essentials. Living in Springfield, Massachusetts, Carol was a lawyer as well as a nun, and Lindsey found stereotype after stereotype riding into the sunset. Her friends were both still nuns and had no intention of changing that, but Carol was uncomfortable staying in Community now that she knew she wanted to be active as a lesbian.

Lindsey had a million unanswered questions about everything Carol was telling her, but Danny wandered over and the conversation became less personal. They went back to the murder. It had been the topic of conversation throughout the restaurant that night. Danny and Lindsey had spent the early part of their shift comparing theories about the murder they overheard at their tables. Odds were running slightly in favor of a drug-related explanation, but some of the men had ominous theories about jealous lovers and college fraternity hazings. Lindsey gave Danny the prize for the evening when one of his tables started insisting the murder was committed by a disaffected wife whose gay husband hung out in P-town to get away from her and the kids. Pretty depressing stuff, they all agreed.

Walter had been quiet all night. He stayed away from the general gossip, but Lindsey saw him talking with the lesbian who owned the boutique up the road, and then again with the two gay men who ran the leather shop at the other end of town. She wondered if it was different for them—what did they have to think about first? Being gay or being business owners who relied on gay customers?

"Have they identified him yet?" Lindsey asked Danny. She'd seen Jose Alfredo come in earlier and wondered if he'd brought news.

"No. At least I don't think so."

"Was he Latino? What did Jose Alfredo say?" she demanded.

"He was definitely not white, but the police aren't releasing anything. We got that from a nurse who works with the doctor who did the autopsy."

"Is it definite it was a gay-related crime?" Carol asked Danny. "Did he really have that word written—I mean . . .carved—on his chest?"

"He really did," Danny said grimly. "And the nurse said his testicles had been cut off. She didn't know if he'd been tortured while he was alive or if that was mutilation after the fact. For the fun of it," he added bitterly.

"We have to do something, Danny," Lindsey insisted. "I talked to Ellen about having some sort of demo or memorial thing. I don't know exactly what. But we have to let people know we noticed that this thing—this hate crime—has happened."

"Maybe we could use the Unitarian place down the street," Carol suggested. "I've heard there's a lesbian minister there who's trying to promote community things."

"That's right," Danny agreed. "She's opened the church up to several of the AA meetings and now the AIDS support groups meet there."

"How do you know about her?" Lindsey asked Carol. She'd been in town for three weeks and hadn't heard this news yet. But then, she hadn't exactly been looking for a church to attend either.

"Rachel is a friend of Andrea and Maureen's. They all belong to a national group of religious lesbians who meet several times a year." She didn't seem to find this news surprising, but Danny and Lindsey stared at her for a moment. "I'd be glad to go and talk with her tomorrow about it, if you want."

"Great," Danny was enthusiastic. "Maybe a couple of us ought to go with you. Kind of figure out what we want to do."

Carol was nodding and Lindsey remembered she'd invited Ellen to help plan the demo part, so in a few minutes they were a delegation of four.

And then it was eleven, and Lindsey was free to slip her arm around Carol's waist and guide her out of the restaurant and down Commercial Street. It was a more sedate street than it had been twenty-four hours earlier, Lindsey thought, as if the town itself was a little stunned by the brutal murder.

The air on the pier was warm, the moon hanging behind a thin haze gave off a gentle light, and even the waves themselves were less insistent than they had been the night before. Lindsey listened to Carol's voice murmuring only a few inches from her ear and gave herself over to the warmth tickling her heart.

"It's not that I couldn't be a nun and be a lesbian," Carol was saying. "Lots of women are, have been for centuries. But I want a home, a partner, a family of my own. I didn't know that when I entered Community life. Andrea is a theologian, and she says celibacy doesn't have a lot to do with sex but with commitment. When you're in Community, you've made a commitment to the group. You can have sex, but your partner can't become the primary focus in life. I think that would be hard for me."

"Hard? I think it would be impossible," Lindsey agreed. Everything Carol was saying was new to Lindsey, totally foreign. "I thought being a nun meant you didn't have sex," she confessed.

"Most people think that. It's usually what happens because anything else is too emotionally difficult. But not always. We don't all want the same thing from intimacy, that's what Andrea says."

She'd at least heard that part before, Lindsey reflected, remembering Ra's amusement at her last night, as her soothing voice reminded Lindsey that we don't all want the same thing from sex, not each time anyway.

"Were you . . . have you?" Lindsey stuttered, then stopped. No. She wouldn't ask it. What did it matter whether Carol had been lovers with a woman yet.

"I tried." Carol read her question and answered ruefully. "I fell in love twice in the convent. The first time she was sent to Peru as a missionary before we had time to get too involved. The second time

I fell in love I decided to apply to law school a thousand miles from Springfield. I thought distance would fix me. But I knew this commitment to Community wasn't going to work when I fell in love again in law school, and there was no place left to run to." Carol paused and Lindsey wondered if the story was finished. Where is this woman now? She wanted to know but was afraid to ask out loud.

"I couldn't make up my mind what I wanted," Carol admitted slowly. "So she didn't know whether I'd choose her or my other life. She left when she felt she was getting too serious."

"And today you took your ring off to see what it felt like to walk around without it?" Lindsey guessed.

"I think that's it. It's like I've been married for eight years. I'm not sure who I am without that...identification. Who is Carol Whittier when she's not a nun? I have to do this now, before I'm thirty. I think it's harder to make changes after you get more settled."

Lindsey nodded her silent agreement. Yes, it was better to have things figured out before you were thirty.

Carol was leading the way now, walking toward the end of the pier, toward the piling where Lindsey and Ra had been the night before. Lindsey knew Carol was oblivious to the meaning of this place, but she was reluctant to revisit it quite so soon. She stopped, pretending to look over the edge of the pier into the water.

"Did you...are you ready to go back?" Carol's voice was hesitant.

"Oh, no. I just—" Lindsey couldn't think of a thing to say. Standing this close to Carol, she could smell the scent of her hair, remember the feel of her lips brushing the other woman's forehead on the beach that afternoon. Why was she so tongue-tied now? Why didn't she do what every inch of her body wanted to do and move that one step closer into an embrace?

Suddenly, Carol did what she had been doing all week in the freedom of this new environment—she threw her natural caution into the breeze blowing off the ocean and put her arms around Lindsey.

Lindsey's lips were waiting. Lindsey's heart was waiting. She felt something in her melt away, some fear, some hesitation she had been carrying with her since Belle left. They kissed slowly at first, lips exploring the contours of a face, tasting the skin, breathing in the scent of a new person. Once again her bare thighs were touching Carol's.

She felt her hands begin to explore the velvet-smooth skin under Carol's blouse. She wanted to see this woman naked, wanted to explore her body inch by inch, everywhere. Her fingers traced the length of Carol's spine, up from the waist to the back of her neck, down again, past the waist this time, beneath the shorts to her tailbone, to her firm ass.

"Oh, my." Carol moved away from the kiss and took a deep breath.

Lindsey's hands did not retreat. She waited for Carol to come back.

"Lindsey, can we go to your place? I'm sharing a room with Andrea and Maureen, and they're both home tonight."

Lindsey was surprised. Who was seducing who, she wondered. Wasn't she supposed to be the experienced dyke? Make the first serious move?

And then she was embarrassed. "I don't know what to say. . ." she started.

"Just say yes," Carol interrupted, her lips fluttering over Lindsey's eyelids like butterflies.

"Yes," Lindsey breathed the word, answering the real question without hesitation. "It's just that I don't have my own place either," she explained. "I share a room with Angie in a very small apartment. Goddess. This is awful."

Carol was laughing. "It sure is. You'd think we were still in the novitiate. Me, I mean. With some elderly nun looking in on you every minute, even while you're sleeping."

Lindsey knew she wasn't going to make love to Carol tonight out here on the pier. And the dunes weren't safe. What a bummer. "I'm not ready to let you go, though," she whispered in Carol's ear. "So get ready for an extended foreplay. I hope we can stand the excitement."

Carol laughed, her head tucked comfortably on Lindsey's shoulder, her hands beginning to move under Lindsey's shirt. "If you can stand it, I can. I was raised on delayed gratification as a principle of virtue."

"Ugh. What an awful thought." But Lindsey was laughing, too, as she waited to see where Carol's fingers would travel next. "I'm not interested in virtue."

Chapter Six

"**O**f course we can have a memorial event if we don't know who he is." Rachel was in the middle of a sentence when Lindsey and Ellen walked into the Unitarian minister's study. They were a few minutes late for their appointment, and Danny and Carol had apparently started without them.

"We were just talking about the parameters," Danny explained. "We want an event that's more political than spiritual."

"I won't agree there is a significant difference," Rachel said, laughing, "but we know what we're talking about. We want to draw the community together around the experience of gayness, all of it—its danger and oppression, its love and specialness."

Lindsey sat down cautiously across from Carol after they exchanged shy, radiant smiles, and looked curiously at Rachel. Who was this minister who could speak so lightly, so fluently, about being gay, who seemed to know something about the contradiction Lindsey was only beginning to experience—the joy and the oppression. Rachel was wearing bluejeans and a T-shirt from the '87 March on Washington. Her short brown hair had probably been combed through with her fingers that morning, and she hadn't spent time on make-up. Wire-rim glasses perched on the end of a short, upturned nose were her only concessions to seriousness—other than her words, which were very serious. Lindsey decided she liked Rachel's looks and settled in to listen seriously.

"Yeah," Ellen was saying, as she nodded at Danny. "Our organizing committee here is two Jews, a serious agnostic," she gestured toward Lindsey—

"And a nun," Carol finished for her, noting Ellen's look of surprise.

"And a Unitarian minister," Rachel added herself to the organizing committee.

"And we don't know anything about the victim, anything for sure, that is," Lindsey reminded them. "He'll be sort of like the unknown soldier, I guess."

"That's not a bad place to start in thinking this through," Rachel suggested. "What we want to say about him is that—whoever he was, gay or straight, Hispanic or not—he died with the word FAG on him and he became a symbol of gay oppression, of all those other gays and lesbians who have suffered violence because of homophobia."

It was like Rachel was preaching a sermon, Lindsey thought, but she had never heard a religious person use words that described what she herself was feeling. Across the room, Carol was nodding emphatically at Rachel's words. And yet, Lindsey felt herself watched, found herself catching Carol's eye on her, without realizing that she must have been watching Carol just as closely or there would have been no eye contact. Lindsey never thought of herself as attractive, and so she always wondered what it was someone might be drawn to in her. She had gazed in the mirror over and over again, first in high school, then at college, and what she saw was a plain freckled face with an average-size nose, brown eyes about an average space apart, an average mouth without much lip demarcation. And always the long brown hair that made her look younger than she was, whenever she was doing her self-assessment. Nothing, she always decided as she turned away from the mirror, nothing to get excited about, nothing to make someone stop and take a second look.

What she did not see, in fact, could not be seen well when she was in repose—her body attitude, a stance that set her forward on her feet, set her sprinting toward any goal, even if it was only toward a table she was waiting on. She was eager. Belle had known that, and Carol had seen it that first night in the restaurant. And she was shy. Ra had seen the shyness right away, the blush waiting near the surface, the diffidence that masked Lindsey's eager move toward experience. The blush didn't show in the mirror, either, and so Lindsey thought of herself as rather confident, forward even, in most respects.

And she had no more idea of what attracted her to a woman than she knew her own desirability. She suspected, rather uncomfortably, that she was drawn to beautiful women, women who were physically attractive in the eyes of the larger world—not even the dyke world—and *that* she would be too embarrassed to ever admit. Her embarrassed reluctance kept her from understanding her desire more fully; her reluctance left her, for example, in a mire of unanswered questions about her night out on the pier with Ra. This focus on Carol, Lindsey assumed, would take care of it. Certainly she hadn't wondered even fleetingly last night whether or not Ra would come into the restaurant.

The meeting was winding down now. They were settling on a short candlelight march with one or two speakers at the end. Starting at 11:00 p.m. as all the shops and restaurants were closing, but before people headed home. Dramatic, Ellen insisted, but their energy should be restrained and respectful. And they could close the ceremony with "We Shall Overcome," Carol said, in Spanish and English. "*Nosotros Venceremos*" was simple enough for everyone to at least do the chorus. Friday night was chosen to involve as many people as possible as spectators and participants. They'd have all week to talk it up, put out flyers, get a notice in the Wednesday issue of *The Advocate*. Lisa hadn't wanted to work on the organizing committee, but she'd told Lindsey that Gloria, Sindar, and Evelyn would help with the singing, maybe choose a piece they'd like to do. Ellen was in charge of the march logistics. Danny and Carol were going to work with Rachel on the brief ceremony at the end. Lindsey was pleased. Clearly all of these people had organized things before and didn't have to be told how to begin.

What now, Lindsey wondered, as they filed out of Rachel's office. She was free until she started work at four o'clock and it was really her last free time until her stint at the Feminist Writer's Conference ended on Friday. She didn't want to let Carol out of her sight yet, nor did she want to presume too much. Carol had said she was staying at the Cape forever, but Lindsey suspected it wasn't that long. She hollered good-bye at Ellen who was dashing off to the theater. Danny had already disappeared. She and Carol were walking slowly, neither speaking.

"Did you eat?" Carol asked finally. "In my family, it's what you do when you don't know what else you should be doing, or when you need comfort, or when you're feeling a little confused."

"Sounds like a great tradition," Lindsey smiled, grateful for the suggestion. "Brunch at the Sunshine Cafe?"

They climbed the narrow steps to the second-floor cafe and ducked inside to find a booth with more privacy than the tables on the open balcony. They were being careful of one another this morning, Lindsey noticed, as though they were carrying a fragile container between them, in a kind of body language pantomime that said, yes, this is special and we want to take care of it, not blunder around and lose it or let it go. But what was *it*? They hadn't looked in the container yet; *its* shapes and contours were still unknown.

For breakfast they had the "Are you involved with anyone now?" question, served with discretion. Carol admitted it had been a year since she had been left by the woman in law school. Lindsey made a distinction between sex and involvement, demurring, "I've had sex since the relationship with Belle, but I've never really been involved with anyone." Carol nodded as though she understood what that meant.

Lindsey did not tell Carol she was having sex with Ra. Carol did not tell Lindsey that she had come out here for a vacation because Gina returned from foreign parts last month and wanted to resume their secret meetings in the back stairs closet, nor did she feel compelled to admit that she had actually met Gina there once last week for old time's sake.

Over coffee they agreed on the things that were important to them in a relationship: honesty, of course, above all, and then a sense of humor, Carol suggested, and Lindsey concurred, wondering if Carol would mind that she could never seem to tell a joke. Lindsey valued loyalty—oh, not the kind that was extreme, like in codependency— but someone you could reasonably count on in moments of stress, at those times the world seemed to turn against you. Carol didn't mention that she had never heard of codependency, but agreed loyalty was the basis of a lasting commitment. Neither asked, out loud, whether loyalty to the Community might take Carol back there.

Carol valued intelligence, a well-informed and reasonably political sensibility. Neither mentioned that physical beauty was impor-tant to her, though anyone watching them as they sat talking would have had to acknowledge that each was attractive in a healthy, whole-some sort of way. Carol wasn't a swimmer, Lindsey discovered, but she had been a tennis player in college and still loved racket-ball sports. Carol had heard Lindsey refer to jogging when she talked about going out to the bike path where the murder happened, and so Carol was able to refrain from her usual tirade about how boring jogging was (and joggers, yes, she had occasionally said it).

Being middle class, it never occurred to either of them to mention class as a factor, nor economic stability, nor the freedom to take va-cations or choose to spend a summer working at the Cape.

They were twenty-six and twenty-eight, and they were falling in love. Each was constructing a safe place in her image of the woman sitting across from her, a place where she could open her heart, ex-pose her tenderest parts without being crushed. In the best romances, both in life and literature, these images are close enough to the real person to avoid betrayal by actual events. But it is surely the first tenet of romance that the image we construct of the loved one will be tested, sometimes sooner, sometimes later, but always it will be tested.

Lindsey began talking about her first lover, Belle. Carol listened as if the story were history, not hearing the unresolved tension, just as Lindsey had not heard Carol's indecision about leaving her Com-munity, preferring to think of it as a choice that was made, finished, resolved.

"Belle was my freshman roommate in college." Lindsey drew de-signs with her fingernail in the tablecloth, not knowing how to tell the story. She had not practiced telling it, like Ra had so clearly told her story over and over. "We were both Women's Studies majors from the start. She was the only woman of color entering the program as a freshman. I didn't know what racism was, but I learned fast."

Carol was frowning. "Surely you don't mean that? Can anyone be alive and aware today and not know what racism is?"

"Oh, sure, I'd read about the Civil Rights Movement and Martin Luther King and all. But this was 1980 in a northern liberal arts col-lege." Lindsey was telling the story rapidly, her frustration and anger from those years pushing her forward on her seat, moving her hands in wide gestures like Danny's. "I'm talking about Belle being asked to be on a college-wide panel on abortion to represent the Women's Studies Department when she'd only been at college a few weeks and didn't have a clue what it would mean to be typed as a Black woman who was pro-abortion and connected to *those white lesbians*. Tokenism. That's what I'd missed. And a general level of petty meanness that made Belle's life hell." Her voice went flat with emphasis.

Carol was nodding now. She had found this too, she told Lindsey. Not in the convent, where there were basically no Black women, but in law school. And a woman who had the impulse to rescue, to fix what seemed so obviously wrong, could really get deeply involved before she understood the issues.

Lindsey didn't know what Carol meant about understanding the issues, but she needed to finish her story and plunged ahead. "At first Belle was angry at her family. She'd been raised in a completely integrated setting—schools, family friends, the whole bit. She didn't understand why they hadn't prepared her more for the world."

"It's hard, I think," Carol offered. "I had a Black friend in law school who said something similar. Like you, she was born the year President Kennedy was assassinated. She and the Civil Rights Movement came to her family in the same year, and by the time she was grown up, it was like the battles had been won. At least the most obvious struggles were over, and her parents wanted to protect the children from knowing what they had experienced.

"Maybe it was like that." Lindsey paused, trying to remember what she had known of Belle's family.

"How did you become lovers?" Carol asked, chin resting comfortably on one hand, the other hand tracing a pattern up and down Lindsey's wrist.

"We were around a lot of lesbians, professors and other students. At first, the idea seemed weird and we talked about how we weren't like that. But gradually it became more familiar. Finally, it just seemed the natural thing."

Lindsey stared down at the table for a moment, realizing how much of what happens between two people is private, beyond telling. She had known Belle's father was an alcoholic. Oh, he functioned, kept his job as a state worker in spite of the more frequent absences, the increased use of sick time. Belle didn't stop bringing friends home until she was in junior high school, and it wasn't until high school that he'd started having blackouts and being away for days at a time. Belle would sit up with her mother, worrying, calling, waiting.

And the first time she and Lindsey made love, it all came out with a rush—Belle's insecurity, fear of abandonment, the need for permanence. Lindsey would always carry with her the memory of Belle's arms around her, squeezing, holding, Belle sobbing, "Don't ever leave me, say you'll never leave me, you can't leave me." Lindsey, scared and inarticulate, had promised, of course, and later, when they were both a little more sophisticated about lovemaking and where orgasms took them, they agreed that it was all right to say anything in bed, anything at all, and it wouldn't be more than pillowtalk. Promises were for their rational moments. Bed was a safe place, a place to explore and feel without having to worry about consequences. At least, that was what they'd said.

Lindsey took a deep breath. Where had she been in her story? Oh, yes, racism. Family. "I think Belle had a reaction, sort of, to being angry at her family. She felt drawn back to them, like she needed to make it up to them, even though they didn't know she'd been angry." She gave Carol a rueful smile. "I learned how seldom we do things for other people, even when we think we are. I mean, how could they need her to make it up to them if they never even knew?"

"But she needed to say she was doing it for them, you mean?" Carol was frowning again, not sure she understood.

"Yeah. I think it let her not be responsible. For hurting me. For not finishing her degree. The summer before our senior year she went home to work, and before it was over she was pregnant and married. In that order."

"Wow. That must have been really hard for you. Have you seen her since?"

"No. She wrote me. Explaining she was doing this for her people. She said I would understand, that I was one of the few white people who would understand. For years, I believed her, thought I did understand. I couldn't figure out why I was so sad all the time, though. Then I realized I didn't understand at all. I was furious." Lindsey could smile at the memory now, but when Sheila had first confronted her

last year, insisting that both Belle's excuse and Lindsey's acceptance
of it were crazy, she hadn't been able to smile.

Lindsey shifted in her chair, ready to turn the conversation to
Carol. "How did you ever decide to go into the convent? I thought
that was something women stopped doing in the fifties."

"Why did you want to be in Women's Studies when you went to
college?" Carol countered. "We were both looking for a community
of women. I'm Catholic, and that's where my tradition took me."

"But I wanted to fight patriarchy," Lindsey responded. "You joined
it."

"I know that now, but it wasn't so obvious at the start. What I saw
was a group of women I admired doing work I wanted to do. Good
work, work in the world. I was making the decision to take final vows
when the four U.S. religious women in El Salvador were killed. Did
you ever hear about that?" Carol peered into Lindsey's face, hoping
to read there some understanding of what she was talking about.

This was a test. Lindsey knew it was a test. She had heard about
them, four nuns, wasn't it? She nodded slowly. "Weren't they raped?"
she asked. "Didn't our government have something to do with it?"

"Only with the cover-up," Carol said grimly.

Lindsey sat back in her chair, relieved. She'd passed. She listened
now as Carol talked, remembering how her lips had traced the outline of that face last night in the dark, how her fingers had combed
through the soft, straight hair. She heard Carol talking about making the world over, making a place that was safe for women and children, how she had worked in a shelter for battered women and their
children and learned she needed more tools, needed law school.

Her intensity, her sense that she knew how to make life better for
the people she worked with, drew Lindsey to Carol, but gave her no
clues about why she felt so stirred. Ra was obviously sexy—in her
dress, voice, Ra's whole demeanor said SEX right out loud. And with
Belle, well, it had been love first, and Belle's obvious need of support,
a champion. They joked about Lindsey's white-knight syndrome.
Not that Belle wasn't attractive, she was gorgeous, but it wasn't a
beauty Lindsey had been accustomed to. She had to grow to appreci-
ate Belle's dark skin, the nose that was wider than fashion models'
noses, the hair that was nappy. No other word would describe that

soft, springy hair—no white words were accurate enough.

But Carol? All Lindsey knew was that she wanted to see Carol hungry, off center and wanting. Something about the calm surface Carol presented—it begged to be disturbed, disrupted. And Lindsey wanted to be the one to make that happen.

They said good-bye in front of the cafe, a long, lingering but chaste kiss. Lindsey wandered down Commercial Street toward her house, not in a tearing rush, but aware that work was only an hour or so away.

The sun poured down on the narrow street, washed off the white clapboard houses and pooled in the center of the street. After a moment or two in that light and heat, the noise of the street began to fade, and Lindsey's thoughts were drawn to Belle, not Carol. Talking about her today—it had been a year since she'd told anyone that much about Belle, and usually she managed not to think about her. For a moment Lindsey let herself remember Belle's broad, thin shoulders, how her breasts were high on her chest, her waist incredibly slender. Lindsey loved making that triangle with her hands, moving across Belle's shoulders, down the outside of her breasts to her waist, and then down to the triangle's final point, Belle's warm, dark center. Belle's orgasms amazed her at first. Each one built for a long while and then rocked her whole body with its force.

And at first Belle wasn't sure Lindsey was even having an orgasm, they were so quiet by comparison. "Tell me when you're coming," she'd demanded, the third or fourth time they made love.

Lindsey smiled as she went on walking down Commercial Street, remembering those dark hands on her so-very-white belly, the part just below her bikini suntan, as Belle's hands moved down, teased the curly hair, then moved up again. Belle loved to tease, make Lindsey moan with pleasure when she finally let her hand slide between willing thighs, her finger probe the wet hardening clit.

In their initial lovemaking, Lindsey only came from vigorous rubbing right across her clitoris, the way she had come since she learned to masturbate as a child. That's what Belle did that day she asked Lindsey to tell her when she was coming. And it was easy, since Lindsey was used to this kind of orgasm, knew when it started to build, could tell Belle, panting, "More, there, no, a little higher, that's it, don't stop, I'm going to come, oh, god, Belle, I'm coming now, now."

Suddenly, a barely familiar dark face smiled into Lindsey's, and a hand reached out to stop her as she marched oblivious up Commercial Street.

"Lindsey, I'm glad to find you. Lisa told me I should talk with you about the song on Friday night." Sindar smiled for a moment, then looked seriously at Lindsey.

"Uhhh. Right." Lindsey flushed, finally recognizing Sindar's face as she came back with difficulty from her reminiscence. "Right. It's great you're willing to help out. We, uhh," she tried to collect her scattered thoughts, "we decided on a candlelight march, with not too much speaking. We want to close with a song the whole crowd can sing, but we thought you might want to do one too." There. She thought that about said it.

"Where will you begin this procession?" Sindar was nodding thoughtfully.

"Up at the P-town monument. We'll go over to Commercial and down. It won't be long, but it ought to have an impact . . . all the candles and stuff."

"Yes. How would it be if we opened the procession with song and drumming? Brought people together to begin? Our music is more joyful and militant. I think it would be better to start that way. We will be free then. It is our break between sets."

"That sounds perfect." Lindsey's enthusiasm was not forced. She could see the sense of what Sindar was saying. It would be perfect, a way to let people know something was happening, draw more people in, maybe.

They chatted for a moment, and when Lindsey was ready to move on, she saw that Sindar had not finished. She waited.

"I wanted to ask you something," Sindar seemed shy now, not as sure of herself as she was a moment ago when they talked about music. Lindsey stooped to catch the words of this short, quiet-voiced woman. "I want to walk on the dunes with you some night. Will you walk with me in your dunes?"

Her voice lilted in Lindsey's ears. She heard the invitation. But surely Sindar was only talking about a walk, surely she meant nothing else. Lindsey nodded again. Of course she could walk in the dunes with this woman. She bent down as Sindar opened her arms for an embrace, a friendly hug. "I'd like that," she said. "Let's do it after the candlelight march is over. Some night next week when you're free."

While Lindsey continued up Commercial Street, Danny was just finishing a long encounter. It had begun as a breakfast date after the meeting at the Unitarian Church, become brunch, and then moved into late lunchtime. Now he was walking out on the pier as though he had some purpose in mind. He pushed past the tourists coming off the whale-watch boats, sunburned and boisterous, past the long lines of prospective whale-watchers waiting to board for the end-of-the-afternoon trips. He ignored a car inching its way up the dock that wanted to pass him, until it actually nudged him and he stepped aside, a look of irritation on his face.

When he reached the end of the pier, however, he seemed to have no goal. He stood for a moment at the water's edge, hands in his shorts pockets, idle. He stared vacantly out at the ocean, looking east in the direction of Safe Harbor, the back of which was not visible even from this outer vantage of the pier. He shaded his eyes with his hand, trying to cut the glare of light off the water as he stared toward town. Finally, he shrugged, his shoulders dropped again. Oblivious to the activity of the fishing boats unloading around him, he stared and stared. Finally a husky dockhand walked over and said something to him, something that made Danny flinch and stalk angrily back toward the tourists.

He had spent the morning with Jose Alfredo, become involved in a conversation that seemed to trap him between his ideals and a very healthy sense of self-preservation.

"Help me, Danny, you have to help me," Jose pleaded, and Danny was not someone who could ignore a plea like that. "I want to quit using, I got to quit using, or I'm a dead man. Believe me. I know that."

Wasn't this what Danny had been wanting to hear? All week he'd talked to Jose, pulled him along to the local AA meetings—meetings that were as much for addicts as alcoholics. One drug or another, it's all the same, that's what they said to one another. Keep coming back. The seed gets planted. One day at a time, just keep clean one day at a time.

Danny knew all the rules, all the truisms. For weeks, months, when he was first trying to get off the drugs and booze, he'd gone to meet-ings and sneered at what he was hearing. Don't get involved with newcomers, don't get sexually involved in your first year sober. Danny didn't know anyone who'd followed that guideline. Certainly not himself. Not at first. He thought he knew too much. He was differ-ent. Nobody who knew anything about gay men's culture would have set *that* as a tradition. And so he crashed. Not once, not twice, but a dozen times at least. Real crash-and-burn stuff. He started day one of sobriety over and over, each time the quick fuck turned into ro-mance and then fizzled. He'd put in three years like that between col-lege and graduate school, three years that convinced most people who loved him that he was lost, convinced those who only knew him a bit that he was worthless.

Finally he'd had enough. He'd done it his way and it didn't work. He came back humble. Quiet. He listened to what the guys with some clean time were saying. Six months clean and sober got him into the Harvard M.B.A. on his college grades and the recommendation of a professor in the AA program who had watched him, who thought he *could* do it. And for a whole year in grad school he'd proved to himself he could do it. Now, a year and a half sober, he wanted to prove it to someone else.

Jose was different. Danny knew he was a special one from the start, the first night he saw him at a meeting. He beat out about ten guys who went over to the newcomer after the meeting, and they went for coffee. The rest, as they say, was history. Jose was incredibly spe-cial. They'd been tight together for ten days and hadn't even had sex. Not that they couldn't have. Not that Danny would have let on to anyone that they weren't lovers. What was the difference? Danny knew desire when he saw it in a man's dark eyes, in the vein throb-bing steadily at the side of his neck, in the hands that were constantly reaching for his shoulders, the arm wrapped around his neck.

But Jose was an addict. He came to the meetings, but he was still using, still trying to get clean. And as an addict, he was a dealer, a conduit between the supplier somewhere out there in the ocean and all those recreational drug users on vacation at the Cape, all those users who would buy a little extra, take it back to Boston, to New York. It was a fantastic trade out here on this farthest little spit of land,

Jose said, fantastic how much got sold here.

"Danny, I got to get free of it. They say if I take this one last ship-ment, I'm done. They'll let me be. But if I take this one, I'm gonna use again, you know I am, man. Coke wasn't even your thing. You won't use. Just pick it up for me when it comes in. Tonight. At the boatslip behind the restaurant where you work. I'll tell you where to leave it. That's all you have to do."

"Jose, the stuff kills people. If I help it come in here, I'm responsible."

"Yeah, amigo, it kills people. It's killing me. Help me."

He should walk away, Danny knew he should. He sat across the table from Jose Alfredo's pleading eyes, despair settling down across his broad shoulders, and nodded.

Chapter Seven

Life is a comedy. At least some days that's the only excuse that makes sense to me. I came home right after work on Monday night, prepared to head straight to bed since I had to report at 9:00 A.M. for kitchen duty at the local high school where the Feminist Writers Conference was being held. The women weren't staying at the high school, mind you, that was where the workshops took place, and the readings at night in the only real auditorium in P-town. For the rest, the resources of the whole town were available, and according to Angie and Lisa—who were hanging out in our living room when I got home just before midnight—*they* were making full use of the facilities. *They* did not include the ordinary everyday women who were taking the workshop, of course. *They* were the heavyweight feminists, the ones who had made it in the big time and had *all* appeared at least once on Donahue or Oprah.

"She's a fascinating woman, Lisa," Angie was protesting as I walked in. Angie managed the African and South American import store in town, and the author of five books on feminist witchcraft theory and practices had apparently spent some time browsing in the store, chatting with Angie. "She knew the history of some of the masks in the store. Really heavy stuff about healing and rituals."

"But her books are awful," Lisa insisted. "Have you read any of that crap? About how we all create our own reality. Like the shit in the world isn't really out there and if we just ignore it, it won't kill us. No oppression. And racism is a figment of *my* imagination?"

"Tell that to the corpse they found out there on the beach," I said, flopping down on the sofa but not really sure I wanted to join this conversation. "What I don't understand is why someone who isn't a writer is being featured at a writing conference. She doesn't call herself a writer, does she? I mean, isn't she sort of like the Jeanne Dixon of the feminist set? Horoscopes? That sort of thing?"

"I think you're both being very unfair," Angie huffed defensively. Apparently talking with this woman for a quarter of an hour had made them fast friends. "Morningstar Moondaughter is a major voice for women today. Her writing reaches women who wouldn't read that more esoteric stuff."

"Like poetry and fiction, you mean?" Lisa was scathing. "I think you mean *her* writing is esoteric. It doesn't reach women who aren't white, middle or upper class, and looking for some easy way to deal with their guilt."

Angie became very quiet and dignified. "You may be right about some of the women who read her work, Lisa, but a writer is hardly responsible for who reads her work or what they do with it." Lisa started to protest, but Angie was on a roll. "And this woman has had life experiences that lift her above that kind of criticism."

"Oh, yeah?" Lisa was suspicious. "Like what?"

I was curious, too. This might be juicy.

"One of the masks in the store really resonated for her." Angie stressed the word *resonated* by making it sound almost French. "She said that wasn't unusual. What she's come to understand as a result of her spiritual work is that her spirit, her personality, has lived many lives. She was probably recognizing that mask from a past life."

"I don't get it," Lisa said bluntly. "What does that have to do with her apolitical and irresponsible writing?"

Angie was very superior now, almost gentle as she explained to Lisa, "Don't you see, Morningstar was a woman of color in a past life. At some very deep level, she *understands* that experience."

"This white woman says she can't be racist because she was a sister in a past life?" Lisa's voice was dangerously low and intense. "Is that what you are truly sitting there telling me, Angie?"

I was worried. Lisa was more upset than I had ever seen her, and Angie, in spite of having known Lisa for years and argued with her on a regular basis since second grade, clearly had no idea what might be wrong with what she was telling Lisa. I myself was thunderstruck. All of my rescue instincts were useless. I opened my mouth, but I couldn't think of anything to say to save the day.

Not that Lisa needed help right now. Her voice started low but began to rise, louder and louder. "She was a woman of color in a past life, so she understands what my life is like today sitting here in this living room in the U.S.A. listening to this kind of shit. Fuck it, Angie. I was a rutabaga in a past life," Lisa was shrieking now, "and that doesn't give me rights in the rutabaga liberation movement."

Angie's look of calm superiority did not budge. I had to admire how, when she got an idea into her head, she was willing to stick with it to the bitter end.

"Look, Angie," I was ready to try, "what if a woman who was married and had all sorts of heterosexual perks, like health insurance from her husband's employment and community support for her relationship and—you know, she sees herself in every movie, book, TV show. All that stuff." For a minute I racked my brain. I knew there were other perks to being heterosexual, but I couldn't seem to remember what they were. So I plunged on.

"What if she told you she understood your oppression as a lesbian today because she'd made it with a woman in a past life in China in the fifteenth century. Would you be impressed with her compassion? Tell her she didn't need to work on her homophobia anymore because clearly she'd suffered enough? Tell her not to feel guilty about all her privileges?" I was really getting into it, could feel myself heating up to the argument.

Angie's facade was starting to slip, but she wasn't giving up. "Why don't you go to Morningstar's lecture and ask her about it yourself," she urged, a little nervously I thought. "We didn't have that long to talk, and the implications of her spiritual development are fairly complex."

"It doesn't seem complex at all to me," Lisa interrupted, "just racist."

"Probably that is because I have not been able to adequately describe her position in this atmosphere of conflict and hostility." Angie had drawn herself upright on the couch and was using her whole body to emphasize her position, but she still looked vulnerable to me, unsure of herself. Like her mask had slipped briefly, and she wasn't aware of it.

For a moment I thought Lisa was about to pounce on Angie, but she got up instead and headed for her bedroom, muttering something about Angie's past lives under her breath.

Now Angie was ready for me. "Lindsey, I think you'll have a different understanding of this after you hear Morningstar yourself. She's really quite impressive. I may try and get someone to cover for me so I can go to her lecture Thursday night." The mask was back in place now that Lisa had left.

Angie was clearly enamored, and there was no point arguing. Besides, I wanted something from her this weekend, and fighting with her wasn't going to get it for me. Angie had spent a few nights out of the house recently. None of us had any idea where she was sleeping, or who with: Angie wanted to know everything and reveal nothing. But I was thrilled. I didn't care about the details because it meant it wasn't me Angie wanted, even if I still didn't know why she was so anxious for me to be doing safe sex. What I wanted was a schedule of her sex life so that Carol and I could plan on having the bedroom to ourselves on Friday or Saturday night. Now was not the moment to ask, however. I was too tired. And the next day was going to come too soon.

I went to bed shaking my head over the notion of past lives, and I went to work the next morning still wondering. As I peeled and grated what felt like a thousand carrots for the famous writers' carrot salad, I wondered whether I had peeled carrots in a past life or if I had, in fact, been someone famous. Angie said you could begin to get a sense of your own past lives if you touched down to what felt most "natural." I definitely preferred having someone pay attention to me, and I don't really like to be overlooked. But then, I don't know anybody who does, so does that mean we've all been emperors or high priests in some other life?

Enough of that silliness, I thought, when *my* heroine strolled through the kitchen, nodded and smiled at all of us peons, and casually grabbed a peeled carrot from my pile. Dexter Williams herself. Now *she* was a writer. Five novels, each one more stunning, more intricate than the last. We had talked in my women's studies classes about how you could watch her craft grow in each book, and we said that if she'd been white, she'd have won a major prize by now. Her sixth novel was due out soon. Women who knew were saying, "Maybe this time...."

Dexter stood in the kitchen for a moment, chatting with the conference organizer, a woman who looked like an older version of Angie—heavy, tall, large-boned and breasted, with frizzy light-brown hair that sprayed out around her head like she'd just been in a high wind or had an electric shock. Next to her, Dexter looked trim and fit. Her dreads had been replaced this year with a close-cropped afro, and I thought, as I eyed her carefully from a distance, that her hair looked a little greyer than in the last picture on her book jacket.

Danny had filled me in on Aretha Shore, the conference organizer, when she'd come into the restaurant one night. Like a lot of people, she'd lived a few lives—in this lifetime, I mean—before she ended up settled in P-town. In one of them she'd been married to a stockbroker in NYC; in another she'd been the head of a lesbian survival center, a separatists' back-to-the-land group in northern California. While she'd done that she'd been a poet, not a bad poet, either, Danny said, though we never read her stuff in women's studies. Now she was director of a retreat center for writers on the Cape during the off-season, the nonsummer months when the Cape was quiet and the notion of retreating here didn't seem ludicrous. I guessed that Danny had heard all of this at one of his AA meetings, but he was careful not to say how he knew it.

"I saw Morningstar Moondaughter out on the beach yesterday," whispered one of the other food-prep flunkies. She was peeling potatoes for tomorrow's potato salad. "She was at the dyke beach and she was *topless*. What do you think that means?"

"That she likes the sun?" I answered with a question, not sure what was being asked.

"Do you think she's finally coming out as a lesbian?" Her tone was hushed, as if we were discussing something sacred.

I confess, my first response was *I hope not*, but I kept that one to myself and just shrugged.

"Her last book was so...gender free," my table mate reminisced. "Even the sections about enhancing your sexual gyre—"

"Your what?"

"You know, your center of sexual energy. Morningstar has renamed some of the more patriarchal concepts. And in this latest book she only refers to your *partner*. It seemed to me something must have brought her to greater awareness."

I certainly hoped so. "If she's a lesbian now, why doesn't she just say so?"

"Oh." The peeling stopped, and she looked shocked. "She has such a large following. Among *all* women. I'm sure she wouldn't want to, you know, alienate anyone."

"Yeah, but if lesbians read her books while she was heterosexual, why won't straight women read her books when she's lesbian?" It wasn't a real question. I knew the answer. Homophobia. But this Morningstar woman seemed to be part of the problem.

"Probably for the same reason *she* doesn't admit she's got a woman lover now," said my friend snidely, nodding at Dexter. O.K. Low blow. It was time to find work at some other table.

We served a small lunch for the organizers and teachers at the conference, an illustrious group of eight women in all. Five writers and three local logistics people. Morningstar, Dexter, Ruth Katz, the columnist and essayist, Janine Johnson, the songwriter who'd created quite a sensation a few years ago by refusing to change her last name to something-daughter, and Margaret Green, one of the academy's most famous out lesbian poets. At least one they were willing to hire to teach *and* sometimes willing to recognize as being worth studying. Sometimes.

The participants, the 200 women who were going to be absorbing wisdom from this illustrious crew, had been arriving all week, and the first session was due to start at 2:00 P.M. I could feel the excitement building as I took the pitcher of herbal iced tea around the table for refills.

Suddenly I saw Rachel, the Unitarian minister, come into the nearly empty cafeteria and stride over to our table. She waved me toward her but went up to Margaret Green and touched her shoulder.

"Rachel," Margaret said with a lot of enthusiasm, standing up and giving Rachel a major hug, right there at the table. I thought they'd probably met before. "How fantastic to see you. When you called last

night, I thought it was too good to be true. My favorite dyke minister given a pulpit in Provincetown. There is justice in this life after all."

They were laughing and hugging and kissing, and I wasn't sure at
all whether Rachel had meant for me to come over or not. I stood
there indecisively, pitcher in hand, wondering if they had been lovers
once. I always wonder about that when I see older dykes who seem
so comfortable with one another's bodies when they say hello. The
way they kiss and hug and hold onto one another ought to be sexual, but it's not. It seems more like a habit, and I wonder how they
got the habit, as it were, and whether I'll ever have that kind of com-
fortableness with someone I'm not lovers with. I can't imagine it with
Belle, but then she's not being a lesbian just now. Face it, I can't imagine even saying hello to Belle from across a room.

"Margaret," Rachel was saying then, "I want you to meet Lindsey
Carter, one of the people I told you about last night."

Margaret turned toward me, her hand reaching for mine, and she
was still smiling. I tell you, I've seen this face staring out at me from
new book jackets every other year since I was a kid in junior high
school, and I'd never seen it smile before. She is such a serious person, this Margaret Green, that's what those photos said to me, the
reader. And her poems. Gloom and doom and struggle and strife.
Sometimes sex, but always in the context of a struggle. How can two
women be together in a misogynist, homophobic world? And every poem I had to read with a dictionary next to me. So I was a little
startled to be called out of my anonymity by Rachel and introduced
to this laughing, relaxed dyke.

"You're one of the march organizers," Margaret was saying to me.
"Rachel told me what happened, and I think what you're doing is
so important."

"I called Margaret last night to ask her to read a poem at the end
of the march," Rachel explained to me.

"That's fantastic," I said, really impressed. "We're opening with the
Kingston Sisters drumming and chanting. What a great closing."

"There's just one problem, Lindsey," Rachel said, drawing Margaret
and me away from the table and lowering her voice. "I wanted you
to know about this, both of you, right away." Her face was serious
now, and I wondered what it could be.

Rachel drew a deep breath. "When I got to the office this morning there were three threats on the answering machine. Three different voices, I think. They all said there would be violence and more death if we went ahead with this march."

I was stunned.

"Wow," Margaret said. "Guess you hit a nerve this time, Rach."

"About our march?" I was incoherent. "How could they mean our march? We haven't even gotten the advertising up yet. Nobody knows about what we're planning, do they?"

"It's us, all right," Rachel said grimly. "They were very specific. I saved the tape for the police to listen to. We've taken the notice to the paper, even though it won't be out until tomorrow. And we've talked to people, I guess. But you're right, it's not well known yet."

"Maybe that will make it easier for the police to track these threats down," Margaret suggested.

"Maybe." Rachel looked doubtful. "I wanted to let you know. I mean, I invited you to read a poem, not risk your life. You might not want to read under the circumstances."

"Rachel." The word was spoken softly, laughingly. "It's Margaret. You remember me?"

I thought I knew what she meant. This was the poet who'd had rocks thrown at her at a demo in South Africa, been forced out of the country, finally, for her anti-apartheid writing, and jailed here in the good old U.S. for protesting U.S. corporate involvement in supporting apartheid. Quite a journey from her introduction to the African continent as a Peace Corps volunteer in the early sixties.

"Just thought I'd give you the chance for a quiet week out here at the Cape," Rachel smiled.

"I do think we need another meeting of our organizing committee," she said, turning to me. "We have to figure out how risky this really is going to be and if we can go ahead." Rachel raised a hand to stop my protest. "And if we are going ahead, we'll need another committee to organize the peacekeeping crew."

I went back to pouring herbal iced tea, but my pulse was racing. Partly this was beginning to feel familiar to me. Not the death threat stuff. I put that right out of my head so it wouldn't totally freak me out. I mean, it couldn't be serious, could it? I mean the other excitement, like in college when we'd get the whole women's studies group together around some injustice. A lot of times the issues had been pretty abstract, like a woman professor not getting tenure in her department or something, but once it had been a question of violence. A professor in the Art Department had come on to one of the visiting Asian students, and when she resisted, he tried to rape her. No one would do anything: the deans, the president said it was her word against his. And her English wasn't perfect, so maybe she'd misunderstood him, they said. Somebody was misunderstanding, but it wasn't Ling. We turned out the entire female half of the student body over that one and some of the more enlightened men, too. He denied it all, of course, but after a couple semesters, he took his tenure and moved to another college. What I remembered most was the rush I got marching down the central campus street, shouting, *Hey, hey, ho, ho, Professor Bertram's got to go*, singing "Fight Back," and choruses of "We are angry, marching women." And we were wave after wave of women saying with our bodies, *This is the line, he crossed it, he's got to go.*

This march would be different, more solemn, but the purpose was the same. We were drawing the line, fighting back. We were saying, this is our community, these are our standards, and we won't settle for less.

I missed the opening session of the writing conference. We were rushing to get food ready for dinner for the assembled couple of hundred participants. But the energy of women streaming into the dining room that evening was high, high, high. I caught a glimpse of Aretha Shore across the room, and she looked even more supercharged than she had at lunch—her hair was sending frizzled energy in all directions. I gathered from what women were saying as they filed past the steam table that each of the writers had presented something about her workshops so the participants could divide themselves up and choose what to focus on during the day. Lots of them would be invited to read in the evenings after each of the "stars" did a reading.

"Oh, I could never do that," one of them laughed nervously to her friend as she took a plate of roast chicken and green beans from me.

"Imagine having to read and let people judge your work right after they've heard Morningstar."

"Or Margaret," her friend gushed, nodding agreement as they moved on toward desserts.

I thought that was a funny concept. I hadn't imagined that writers read their work to an audience to have it judged, but because they had something to say they wanted others to hear. I shrugged. Probably I was being naive again.

I was surprised to hear that the name of a writer who wasn't at the conference kept cropping up again and again from the other side of the steam table. How was Beryl Chatham connected to all this? She was the lesbian writer whose books you were most likely to see out at Herring Cove during the summer. The author of the quintessential lesbian romance series. If you hadn't read at least five of the seventeen in-print Beryl Chatham romances by the end of your first summer in P-town, they took away your Lesbian Identity Card. At least that was what Ellen told me the first week I was out here. I hadn't finished one yet and was in some danger of mailing my Lesbian Identity Card back without waiting for them to ask me for it. Something about the level of dialogue and lack of plot offended me. "*Deidre, I have to tell you this right now. It can't wait. I've never been so. . .oh, I don't know how to say it. It's your. . .cheekbones.* [Heavy breathing.] *They are so. . .compelling.*" Frankly, I'd rather read Angie's het romances. I expect less of them.

Beryl Chatham, it seemed, as the gossip filtered back, was making a surprise visit to the conference. Not to give a workshop on how to write—I heaved a sigh of relief when I heard that—but as a gesture of solidarity with the town and people who were supporting this venture. Beryl Chatham was giving a reading on Saturday afternoon, for free, open to anyone who wanted to attend.

Saturday seemed a hundred years away at least. First we had to get past Friday night alive. Tomorrow the paper would come out with our ad telling people about the march and our reasons for calling it. And who knew how many more death threats would be recorded on Rachel's phone machine then? No, I commanded my mind, this is not fruitful speculation. Think about wiping down the food-prep tables. Something nice and centering.

At 9:00 P.M. I clambered back on my bike and wobbled off toward my house. The high school was lit up like it must have looked in the middle of the school year as I glanced back over my shoulder. Twelve solid hours of work had done me in. I couldn't even be interested in what was happening there now. I hadn't had time to think of Carol all day. Not once, I realized guiltily. Except maybe when Rachel had said we needed to have another meeting of our planning committee. I wanted to remember how I felt when her green eyes looked deeply into mine, how my heart raced when our warm legs entwined, when her lips met mine. But my body was heavy and, frankly, there was little energy left in my sexual gyre.

Ellen and I staggered into our committee meeting the next morning at eight. For a moment I was glad no one looked a whole lot more chipper than me. Carol sat in a large chair on the other side of Rachel's office. She nodded at us when we came in, and there was the bustle of taking lids off of coffee-to-go cups, so I didn't notice at first. But as I settled into my spindly chair and took a first sip of coffee, I tried to catch Carol's eye, get a special smile or notice, but she wouldn't look at me. She seemed really involved in listening to Rachel's description of the threats we'd received and doodling on her pad.

Well, maybe she was upset. We were all trying to be cool, like death threats were part of the scene here on Cape Cod. I tried to listen to Rachel, too, but it would have been a lot easier if Carol had smiled at me. I couldn't help it. All of my alarm signals were starting to buzz.

"I invited Don Slocum to come to our meeting to talk with us about the situation," Rachel was saying, as a short, stocky man slouched through the door. Slocum was the P-town chief of police. This was getting serious, I thought, and took another gulp of my coffee.

"I told Rev. Smyth I wanted to speak to you folks this morning," he began in a soft voice. "That was even before we got this latest batch of calls."

Wow. There must have been more threatening calls. We were all sitting forward now, listening carefully.

"I want to ask you folks to call this thing off. I could beat around the bush about safety and all, but we're all adults here," he paused and looked around the room, including us all, "and we know you can't do something that will endanger the people you're inviting to come. It's that simple."

I was speechless, but it seemed as though everybody else on the committee had something to say, and they all started to say it at once. Rachel put her hands up in mock defeat. "One at a time, one at a time." And she called on Carol first.

"This is Sister Carol Whittier," she explained to Slocum, stressing the word Sister. It was the first time I'd heard Carol described like that. I wasn't sure I liked it.

"It doesn't seem at all simple to me," Carol said calmly. "We are, it is true, talking about a political event, Chief Slocum. But it is also spiritual in its expression. And as you know, people have always taken risks for that."

"And people have always taken risks for their own liberty," I added quickly, not wanting this to get too religious. "Where would the Civil Rights Movement have been if everybody had gone home quietly the first time there was a threat of danger?"

"People who came to those demonstrations knew what they were bargaining for," Slocum disagreed with me. "I'm talking about a different population and different—what? Assumptions? People come here on vacation. My job is to keep this town peaceful so everybody here has a good time and comes back next year. That's what the people who pay me want." He was letting us know that we weren't among the people he was responsible to.

"I think we'd be willing to have the candlelight walk be a short block or two, Don," said Rachel, beginning to work on a compromise. "Most of the time will be here in the church, and of course you don't have a problem with that." She didn't end that statement with a question mark. I hadn't thought we would be inside the church at all. We would need to have another talk after Slocum left.

Which he did rather quickly after we agreed to talk with him again on Friday and keep him informed of any more threats. I wondered if we might have considered canceling or postponing the march ourselves if we hadn't had Slocum to resist. But without really knowing what had happened, it seemed like we were committed to going forward with our plan.

Danny, I noticed, hadn't said a word all morning. He looked even more exhausted and morose than Carol. I thought maybe he was tired of not getting any sex from Jose Alfredo. It had even occurred to me recently that Jose might not be gay, that it might be something other than sex he wanted from Danny. Danny would have agreed, in part. Danny thought he was helping a fellow addict in his recovery, I was sure, and probably hadn't pushed too hard about the sex, since he couldn't admit that was what he really wanted. How does life get so complicated?

Carol and I, on the other hand, wanted sex. At least I had thought we did, until this morning. But if I couldn't work out a plan with Angie to share our room, we were going to have a very long courtship or would have to rent a motel room for a night somewhere, which neither of us could afford. And now I couldn't even catch her eye across a crowded room. What could have happened in twenty-four hours? What had I done wrong?

Rachel agreed to find extra peacekeepers for the march from some of her P-town regulars, the year-rounders, they call themselves, in contrast to us transient summer people. Our meeting was over, not because we didn't have more to talk about, but because several of us had to go. Danny rushed off to the morning AA meeting. Ellen's play opened Friday night just before the march, so she was in all-day rehearsals. I was late for work, but I lingered a moment, hoping to see if Carol would let me in. I already felt lonely, anticipating—with that empty feeling in my chest—what it might be like to not have Carol to look forward to.

"What's wrong?" I tried to make my voice concerned, gentle, not too demanding, as we walked out of the church.

"I'm sorry." A tear crept down her soft cheek.

Shit. I'd known it wasn't going to be good news, but if she was apologizing before we started talking, it was probably very bad news. I tried not to anticipate her too much. "What are you sorry about?" That had been a rather cryptic hello.

She got the point and gave me a little smile. "For being such an idiot." She shrugged with annoyance. "I'm confused again. I hate being confused. Some other women from my Community came out here yesterday, and now. . .oh, I don't know, it's just confusing," she ended irritatedly.

"They want you to stay with the Community?" I ventured, not really believing what I was hearing. She had sounded so sure of herself, her decision to leave.

"I don't know. Yes. No. I don't think I can talk about it now," she was angry with herself, and I didn't want her to be angry with me, too.

"It sounds like you need some space," I offered magnanimously. That was easy. I didn't have time to see her until after the march on Friday night anyway. "Maybe we could plan on spending some time together after the march on Friday? Do you think...could we talk then?" I wanted to ask her if she'd spend the night with me if I got Angie out of the way, but this didn't seem the moment.

I was rewarded with a smile that looked at me for the first time that morning. She seemed relieved that I wasn't asking her for anything major right away. "I'd like that," she said, placing her soft lips on my cheek, then pulling away with a wave. "See you then."

Chapter Eight

Friday morning came with a bleak drizzle. Lindsey groaned and turned over in bed when her alarm beeped, wishing she could stay there forever. One open eye told her this might not be a random shower, that the Cape could be socked in good, maybe for days. Hooray. What a great Fourth of July weekend. She wanted to hide out under the covers for at least a week. Last night she had worked again at Safe Harbor after being in the conference kitchen all day. Today was a repeat of that, with the candlelight march to follow it all. Her twenty-six-year-old body felt about eighty-eight as she tried to find a comfortable valley in the lumpy mattress and sink back into the fantasy her alarm had pulled her out of.

In the dream she was in the dunes above High Head Beach with Ra and Joan. Ra was massaging Lindsey's tired feet, her fingers moving gently, firmly around the heel, pulling on each toe. Ra was topless, just like on the beach last weekend, and she rested one of Lindsey's feet between her soft bare breasts as she reached for the other and began to caress it. Dark-haired Joan, meanwhile, had leaned forward and was placing soft kisses on Lindsey's smiling face. She felt the sun on her face, then on her breasts as Joan unfastened her bathing suit top and pulled it aside. Was it the breeze or Joan's soft cheek brushing lightly against her breasts? She could feel Ra's expert fingers moving up her legs, massaging her calves first, then moving toward her thighs. Her clitoris began to tingle with anticipation, as if it had an imagination of its own, as if it knew just where Ra's fingers were heading. Which, of course, it did. Just as Joan's lips clamped firmly around one nipple and began to suck, Ra's finger slid under the edge of Lindsey's bikini leg. Lindsey felt warm and wet and very happy in her anticipation. She didn't need to move or act, it would all happen just the way she liked it. She sighed deeply.

"Aren't you going to work this morning, Lindsey?" Ellen's demanding voice coming through the door to her bedroom pulled her out of the fantasy. Angie was still a lump under the quilt on the other bed.

"How can you be so cheerful and awake?" she asked Ellen in an accusing voice after she stumbled to the bathroom and out to the kitchen for a cup of coffee. "Look at this day. It wasn't meant for anything but sleeping." She was not looking forward to riding her bike out to the high school in this drizzle.

"It will pass," Ellen said cheerfully. "The weatherman said it would burn off by noon. The real big storm won't get here until tomorrow."

"So let me sleep till noon, then," Lindsey mumbled incoherently. Just because Ellen's play was opening tonight didn't mean everyone had to be on adrenalin rush at eight in the morning. "So it won't be raining for the march tonight?" She finally got the import of Ellen's words.

"That's the promise. Rachel's handling last-minute details and said she knows where to find us all if there are any changes."

"Like if the police chief gets nervous again?"

"Yeah, but it's been fairly quiet." No one could figure out why, but there hadn't been another threatening call since the newspaper ad came out, so the police chief had given the go-ahead. It seemed like it would be safe, especially with the crew of peacekeepers Rachel had rounded up.

"Meet you at the monument at eleven, then," Lindsey called to Ellen's departing back.

The drizzle had turned to fine mist by the time Lindsey pedaled out to the high school. The sun was going to try and come through the clouds, she could tell. She was a few minutes late, but this was her last morning, and there was no one who would care when she started the salad prep as long as it was ready by lunch. The air was heavy with salt and moisture, letting her know in its own special way how close she was to the ocean. If she closed her eyes, Lindsey thought for a moment, she could pretend she was biking under water. If she closed her eyes, the voice of reality intruded, she would probably fall asleep again and run her bike into a ditch.

So she let her mind wander back to the dream she'd been having when she woke up. Funny, the dream wasn't about Carol. She'd been thinking about Carol a lot since Wednesday morning, wondering what she meant when she said she was confused, wondering why having more women from her Community visiting the Cape made it harder for Carol to leave. But the dream had been about Ra, who would come back to Safe Harbor tonight, just like she'd said. Lindsey had no doubt about that. And Joan had been in the dream.

It hadn't seemed weird or anything, having two women making love to her. But it was nothing Lindsey had ever done, or thought she wanted to do, so why was she having this fantasy? And why had she been so passive? That question was buzzing around her head like a deerfly.

She'd asked herself the same question after that night on the pier with Ra. Why had she let Ra move her hands back like that, shift her weight so that she couldn't reach up and touch Ra, not even to play with her breasts or feel between her legs to see if she was wet too? Sure, Lindsey liked being made love to, but she liked other things—like leaning over a woman as she ran her hands from breasts to cunt and watching the changes on her face. She liked touching a woman, being bold, plunging her fingers or her tongue deep in her lover's vagina.

Lindsey had learned several things about her fantasy life. She knew she used fantasy to relive moments that had been awkward or gone badly, moments in which she wished she had acted or responded differently. Those moments played over and over again in her mind as she imagined different responses for herself, until she found the one she was comfortable with, the one she hoped she'd be able to use the next time, or the one she hoped she could use to make sure there wasn't a next time. And she knew she used fantasy to imagine things she had never done but might want to try. When she and Belle were drawn to being lovers, Lindsey's fantasy life was way ahead of her, showing her some version of what it would be like to touch Belle, how she could pull her into an embrace, what it might feel like to move Belle's legs apart and bury her head in another woman's cunt.

Lindsey thought she used her fantasy life to preview real life, to imagine herself doing something so that she could then in fact do it. That was why Sheila accused her of not trying things spontaneously. But Lindsey didn't understand yet how fantasy could give her access to her shadow self, the part of her that could imagine things she might never want to do but needed to comprehend. For now, she could only wonder whether her fantasy meant she wanted to see Ra again, wanted to make love with several women at once, or whether it meant anything about her feelings for Carol. No, she rejected that query as she pedaled up the last hill. It couldn't be that. And so Lindsey concluded she had no answer to what her fantasy might predict, without suspecting she might be asking the wrong questions.

She shook her head a little as she coasted up to the bike rack, dismounted, and locked her bike. The salad bar was waiting for her.

Lindsey poured herself a cup of coffee from the urn, made a face at the bitter brew, and took her place at the cutting table. She spread the vegetables out in front of her, a stack of deep aluminum containers on her right. After only four days, she'd gotten into a routine that gave her an hour by herself—surrounded by other workers, but alone with her job. The cook didn't come in until ten, and Lindsey had till then to get the salad bar items out of the way. She'd picked a spot where she could watch what was happening out in the cafeteria. This quiet anonymity suited her fine. No one attending the conference knew her name, and the groupies doing work exchange in the kitchen thought she was standoffish. She'd sat in on two afternoon sessions, but not as a participant. She was too shy and too insecure to think of what she wrote in her journal as writing. And since her first conversation with the Morningstar devotee who hoped for nothing more than to find her idol topless at Herring Cove Beach, Lindsey had just listened and nodded. She'd actually picked up quite a bit of information that way, she realized, as she checked the cafeteria for the usual cast of characters.

At a table near the door to the kitchen was Aretha Shore and her entourage. Never alone, she usually trailed the length of the cafeteria, waving to dozens of people, stopping to make significant comments to important people like Morningstar and Dexter. But Lindsey had been a few minutes late this morning, and she'd missed

Aretha's entrance. Aretha, Lindsey overheard, had been royalty in several of her past lives, which was why she felt comfortable having someone follow her around, pick up the pieces of her life as she dropped them. And why she deserved a different sexual partner every night, Lindsey deduced. Last night's lover was still with her, frail, blonde, and clinging, looking like a ballet dancer who might have done Swan Lake—the enamored and helpless white swan, not the powerful black one.

Across the room, another figure coming through the door caught Lindsey's attention. Margaret Green. Small-boned, but tall and lanky, dressed in bluejeans and a cotton T-shirt, her hair cut short and severe, Lindsey never would have guessed she was fifty-something if she hadn't read all those books. No one noticed her as she wound through several tables to the coffee urn. She paused for a moment after she stirred her coffee, took a sip, looked thoughtfully around her, and then turned to walk toward Lindsey and the kitchen. Waiting for her to come through the door, Lindsey wondered why it was that some people sought attention and others got it. Whenever Margaret Green had something to say, people would pay attention, close attention. Was that why she didn't allow the entourage? Surely she could have had the same kind of following as Morningstar or Aretha. But then they might have gotten in the way of her work, and this was a woman to whom her work was paramount; she left the world no doubt of that.

"Have you counted the carrots you've chopped in the last four days?" Margaret perched on the edge of Lindsey's cutting table and peered into the half-full carrot bin.

"No. What I'm counting right now is the hours until I'm finished chopping."

Margaret nodded. "The weather report says it will be clear tonight. Do you think that's right?"

"It's always hard to tell out here, but I heard the same report. When I biked in just now it seemed like it was lifting." Lindsey scraped a pile of carrots into the bottomless bin. "Did you talk to Rachel this morning? Have there been any more threats?"

Margaret shook her head. "None. Rach can't figure it out. Me neither. Why such a fierce response at first and now nothing? It makes me wonder if they're saving it for tonight."

Lindsey's head came up and her eyes narrowed as she looked at Margaret. In the absence of the threats, she had let go of her fear. Now it came back to her in a rush of adrenalin. Lindsey made sure the knife was very steady before she started chopping again. "Are you nervous?" she asked suddenly, not sure where the question had come from.

"Of course." Margaret answered without hesitation.

Lindsey felt flustered, wished she hadn't asked. She remembered Rachel telling Margaret she didn't have to read and Margaret laughing at her.

"Aren't you nervous?" Margaret's inquiry was friendly as she turned the question around on Lindsey, who shrugged and appeared to think for a moment.

"It's hard to tell the difference, sometimes, between nervous and excited. I wish I could say I'm just excited, but now that you mention it, I think that fluttering in my stomach is more than . . . gosh won't this be fun."

"Right. It would be so much easier if we could just do the things we think it's right to do instead of having to do them in spite of being afraid, or worrying we can't do it well enough, or the dozen other things that usually go through my head at a time like this." Margaret smiled a little ruefully and took another sip of her coffee.

Lindsey was remembering now, wasn't there a poem about being afraid in South Africa? About facing those furious white people and seeing in their faces the face of her own fear?

"What are you going to read tonight? Something about fear?"

"No. But that would make sense, wouldn't it?"

Lindsey nodded. It was nice not to be discounted. To be standing here having this conversation like they were two normal people instead of one who was famous.

"I'm thinking about reading a poem about love, actually. What do you think? It seemed to me that this march is about love, at some important level. Being free to love openly." But Margaret's face was troubled, not settled.

"Yeah. I think that's what it's about. Not being killed because of who you love. But there's something else, too. I don't quite know how to say it. That he's still unknown. That nobody who loved him has come and claimed his body, said *he's one of ours.*" There was a long pause as Lindsey piled the last of the carrots in the container, took it over to the walk-in cooler, and came back to begin topping the radishes. "Then there's the race thing. That he was a person of color, I mean. I don't know what to say about that. I guess none of us do."

"Hmmm." Now Margaret's face had gone really thoughtful. "You're right. White people never think we know what to say about racism, but what we've learned is that we have to say something, even when it's hard, even when it comes out wrong. Thanks, Lindsey," she turned back to Lindsey, not looking uncertain any more. "I needed to hear that."

I was remembering those words that night as I ran up to the monument a little late, wondering how Margaret would find what it was she needed to say. I had a feeling, though, that she would find it. Sindar and her friends had already pulled something of a crowd with quiet, but insistent, drumming. Rachel, Ellen, and Carol were moving among people, handing out candles. Rachel had a batch of armbands to signify the peacekeepers, and she gave me one as I took a candle from her.

"Just walk on the edge of the crowd," she said, "and keep your eyes open for trouble. If anything develops, get word to me." She had a walkie-talkie thing on her belt.

Ellen and the set design crew from the theater had made some cardboard tombstones that said Unknown Dyke and Unknown Faggot on them. I was impressed. They were really dramatic, and they sure made the point.

"They're great!" I told her, and in the same breath remembered to ask, "How was opening night?"

"Not too bad," she looked distracted. "Alan could use some work, but the audience liked it. They're pretty forgiving out here." She laughed a little.

"I know a great understudy for Alan if this guy doesn't work out," I kidded Ellen. "He speaks English pretty good except for the heavy Latino accent."

Ellen looked irritated for a moment, then remembered Danny and his friend and started to laugh.

"So where is he anyway?" We both realized Danny was the only one of our committee not here yet, and from the growing intensity of the drumming, I was guessing we were about to start. Danny had left work when I did, and I assumed we were headed in the same direction, but he was nowhere to be seen.

I swung around the edge of the crowd, careful not to look in the place I'd last seen Carol handing out candles. I'd had an easy talk with Angie. I stopped in her store on my way to the restaurant, and she clearly had something important on her mind, something unrelated to my sex life. "Sure, Lindsey, you can have the room. If I come in, I'll sleep on the sofa. Just leave my quilt in the living room, O.K? That will remind me." She went back to the man and woman standing by the African masks and resumed her hushed, intense conversation with them.

That was fine with me. I was beginning to doubt now that I would ever make love with Carol. I went from anger to indifference to hurt and lonely at least three times a day. I mean, who was this woman, anyway? I hardly knew her. We'd talked once or twice and necked on the pier once. No reason for me to be planning my future with her. But I had been. In just those few short hours, for some reason, I had let my heart be open to her. Closing it again was not going to be easy.

Just then, down the narrow alley leading up to the Monument, a familiar truck caught my eye, black with lots of chrome and spotlights mounted on the roof of the cab. What was he doing here? I crossed Bradford Street and peered down the alley. It was the same truck that had nearly run me over last week. I was pretty sure of that. The hair on the back of my neck actually started to bristle. The suspense novels were right: it could happen. The engine was idling very quietly. This was no truck with a souped-up muffler. Suddenly the passenger door opened, and someone slid out the far side. The window glass was so dark I couldn't see the driver, even when the interior light came on. And then, coming down the alley toward the bush I was standing behind, I saw Danny.

"Danny! Where have you been?" I stepped out from behind the bush and the headlights of the truck came on and spotlighted us for a moment. "Were you in that truck? Did you just get out of the truck?"

Danny looked confused, distressed, for a moment. "No. Uhh, I was cutting through the alley. Why?"

"Oh. I saw someone get out. He must have gone the other direction. Come on." I was impatient now, for I could hear that the rally had started. We stepped aside as the truck pulled out of the alley past us. Why did I still feel the hair on my neck stand up, feel someone's eyes looking at me through that dark glass?

Rachel was welcoming people, saying briefly what the event was about. She talked about the unknown soldier and how he/she came to represent everyone who had sacrificed in the struggle. Then she said that tonight we were claiming the body of the unknown gay man who'd been killed last weekend, claiming him as one of our own by this ceremony. Her words sat heavily on my heart, and I began to realize I was lonely. Looking around the crowd circling the monument's base, I knew I wanted to be with Carol. There she was, not too far off, holding her box of candles and wearing an armband like mine.

I stood next to her quietly for a moment before she realized I was there. We looked at one another, a long serious look, and then she took my hand in hers and held on to it, letting her attention go back to Rachel.

Did my heart soar? No. I stood holding her hand feeling . . . not exhilaration, but something more humble. Relief? Gratitude? and, for the first time since Wednesday, a real sense of hope. We were connected again. Whatever had been missing was back. That was what I felt. "Light your candles now," Rachel was saying. "Light them for one another as a symbol of our connection to one another." And we did.

The march was starting to move out, led by Gloria, Evelyn, and Sindar, followed by Ellen and the cast and crew of *Torch Song* carrying the tombstones. Carol and I separated to be peacekeepers on the edge of the walk, but I felt the thread still connecting us. As I walked down Bradford Street toward City Hall and the turn down to Commercial Street, I looked furtively up every driveway and alley, wondering if I would see the black truck.

The spectators were mostly quiet, watching. Het couples in town for a night of dancing, some families still out after eleven, a lot of tourists gawking who had no idea what it was about as we walked by, shielding our candle flames with our hands. I was surprised how many people I knew who were marching. Quite a few women from the writing conference were there, women I'd only seen before in the high school cafeteria. Margaret had been talking about the ceremony in her quiet way all week. And there she was, toward the front with Rachel and Dexter. Ra, Joan, and Gabrielle had come into Safe Harbor just like they had promised, and now they were walking together in the center of the crowd.

There were more men than I had expected. About half the crowd, in fact. That was good. Danny had done a lot of organizing. I would see him every night at the restaurant, collaring the men who came in to dine, or talking in a low voice with groups of two and three men strolling by on the sidewalk when business was slow. He'd gotten out a lot of the AA community, too, I was willing to bet as I checked out the crowd.

Ra had predicted at dinner there would be a good turnout of men. The event wasn't too frighteningly political, she said; it was only a candlelight vigil, after all. To our relief, nothing had been in the papers about the early death threats. Whatever rumors were around must have circulated quietly and been dismissed as unimportant by those who had heard them and chose to come anyway.

Gabrielle agreed. She said gay men had learned a lot about building community in the last few years. She was talking about AIDS, I knew, but I could still hear Lisa's dismissive words on the beach that day, not believing that white gay men would come to claim this Latino as one of theirs. Probably the crowd was smaller, the feeling less intense, but I was glad this crowd was here, here for Lisa, here for me. Maybe if we kept trying, we could work it out after all; maybe the only thing that kept us from being the community we all talked about and seemed to want was our fear that we weren't enough for one another. There must have been several hundred of us with candles now, walking silently through the streets of Provincetown. I was glad to see Carol a few yards ahead of me, catch a glimpse of her face occasionally in the light of the candle she carried.

The first part of the crowd must have arrived at the church. We at the end were just rounding the corner when I realized the black truck was following us slowly, bringing up the rear of the walk like an escort. It was too late for me to get to Rachel, and what would I have told her? That the hair on the back of my neck stood up when I looked at this truck?

All of a sudden we, too, were in the yard in front of the church. Rachel had set the PA system up there instead of indoors, and now the yard was filled with flickering candles reflecting the faces of the people who carried them.

Then the church doors swung open, and three huge figures, swathed in black cloth, came forward and stood in front of the crowd. Was this an attack? My heart started to thud the panic alarm again. At first all I could see were the huge masked heads, and then I saw the sign they carried: Spirits of Gays and Lesbians Past Join You. Goddess help us, I realized, it must be Angie. The masks were from her store. The three took up a lot of space for a moment, and then Rachel seemed to get over her shock, went up and spoke to the group, moved them slightly to one side, and we were ready to begin.

Rachel said a few words. It might have been a prayer, but if it was she managed to avoid mentioning god at all, never mind this genderless stuff like creator/mother/father. Then Margaret stood up, and Dexter was with her. Margaret wasn't going to read one of her own poems at all, she said, she was going to read the poem of a Latina lesbian living in the U.S., and Dexter was going to read each stanza in Spanish following Margaret. She talked first about the voices we are allowed to hear and those that are silenced by our society. The crowd was very quiet. I was standing at the back, next to Carol, with her hand in mine again. Margaret, it seemed, had found the words she needed.

I was so enthralled by Dexter's rich, sonorous voice rolling out her fluent Spanish, that I forgot for a moment to be a peacekeeper, until my happy concentration was jostled by the crowd being pushed forward from the rear, from the street. I started to say, "Watch it, buddy," to the drunk tourist whose elbow I felt in my back, when I heard Carol's quick intake of breath and a worried, "Uh, oh, trouble."

Coming down the street behind us, forcing bystanders out of the street and into the yard with us, was a huge pickup truck, its muffler rumbling as the driver gunned the engine over and over. A blond teenager leaned out of the window, waved a beer bottle at the church, and screamed, "Kill fags." There was no doubt. This was not a support rally. Behind him was another, equally loud truck with a sign across the hood in crude lettering, Homos Go Home, and behind that another truck. I couldn't see how many there were. Suddenly two motorcyclists in black leather pulled up beside the lead truck, and a siren started to wail. Not a police siren, though we were less than a block from the police station, but a siren from one of the trucks, meant to silence us. Then a horn started, a long blare, and another. Six or seven more motorcycles revved in chorus and wove in and out of the slow moving trucks.

This all happened in thirty seconds or less. By the time I turned back toward the church, looking to see if Rachel was sending me directions, Margaret and Dexter had finished and Rachel was back at the microphone. I doubted she could be heard over the noise, and the crowd at the back was very nervous. Tourists were leaving fast, and I could see some of the people blowing out their candles, getting ready to move. One of the marchers had turned and started to scream at the line of trucks, trading obscenities. Carol and I moved toward some other peacemakers who were joining hands at the rear of the yard to keep the two groups separate.

With my back to the crowd, my eye on the trouble just ahead of me, I could only hear dimly as Rachel tried to start people singing "We Shall Overcome." It was not the song of the moment, let me tell you. Too slow and nervous the way these white folks were singing it.

And then Don Slocum was there. Two police cars, lights flashing, but without sirens, pulled up on the sidewalk between the trucks and the candleholders. Suddenly things were calmer, the honking stopped, and the few remaining trucks drove by silently.

Seldom in my life have I been grateful to the patriarchy. I heaved a sigh of relief but remembered my training. "We could have handled it ourselves," I said, turning to Carol.

"Probably," she agreed, but her face looked relieved.

We faced one another like that for a moment, and then she was in my arms and we were hugging and crying and laughing. What at?

It didn't matter to me at all. I just wanted to stay like that forever. And we did. While the strains of "We Shall Overcome" picked up, then soared around us, we hugged one another. She was murmuring sweet nothings in my ear, softly saying over and over, "I want you, Lindsey Carter. It's you I want, do you hear me?" I heard her. I whispered that I'd gotten the room free tonight, would she go home with me, would she touch me the way she'd promised that night on the pier?

And then it was over and people were leaving. Holding tightly to Carol's hand, I started to move forward. I wanted to see the rest of the committee before we left, thank Margaret and Dexter for their poem. I was finished with my work at the Writer's Conference and didn't expect to run into them again.

Without knowing how it happened, Carol's hand slipped out of mine and Sindar was standing in front of me. She reached up to hug me and, what could I do, I bent over for a hug. "You were wonderful," I told her, "the drumming was fantastic. It did set the tone. I think we were ready, stronger, because of the drums."

"The drums speak in a strong voice when they are needed," she agreed. "Lindsey," she put her hand on my arm and drew me closer to her, "you said we could walk together on the dunes after the march. Will we go tonight?"

I looked at her, speechless. I hadn't said that to her, had I? How could I have, when all I could think about was seeing Carol after the march? I could feel Carol beside me now, could feel her shock as she heard Sindar's words, or at least I imagined I could.

My brain was stammering as I tried to force words out of my mouth. "Sindar, I can't walk with you on the dunes tonight. If I said 'after the march,' I must have meant later this week. I'm sorry." The small woman was looking crestfallen, disappointed, and I hate disappointing people. I reached for her hand and held it in both of mine. "I *do* want to go to the dunes with you some night. Can we go tomorrow night? After we are both finished with our work?"

"That would be good, Lindsey." She was smiling again now. "You will come to the hotel and we can leave when we are finished with the last set, yes?"

"Yes." I would have agreed to anything, I was so anxious to turn around, to find Carol and explain what had just happened, make a joke with her about it. "I'll see you tomorrow night, then, Sindar."

I turned and looked where Carol had been, but she was gone. I saw her briefly across the lawn of the church, walking rapidly toward the street. A short woman with dark curly hair was at her side, holding her hand. I stood and watched them disappear up Commercial Street into the crowd. I didn't know what had happened. But Carol was gone. Gone. And I was standing alone, holding a candle that had blown out in the night breeze.

Chapter Nine

On a quiet Saturday morning a figure on a bicycle pedaled through the rain, splashing the wrong way down Commercial Street. The biker was wearing a rain poncho with a hood that came down over what must have been shorts, leaving an image of a small body with long bare legs. The biker seemed to be headed somewhere quite deliberately, though not in a hurry, weaving in and out of the few tourists who were bustling from shop to shop, trying to pretend this was fun since they couldn't be on the beach. Past the piers and before the shops had thinned out too much, the biker turned left on a small side street, going very slowly now, but still quite deliberate. It stopped in front of an unpretentious guest house with a sign so faded it could barely be seen from the street. The biker walked the bike around into the yard and propped it up against a shrub, then threw the hood of the rain poncho back off her head and rang the doorbell.

The door opened, and Lindsey stepped inside at the invitation of the woman with short blonde hair who stood in front of her.

"Can I help you?" she asked, friendly.

"I'd like to talk with Carol Whittier, if she's up," Lindsey said in a low voice.

"Gee, she's up. And gone. She left for Springfield early this morning. Something came up, I guess. She had a reservation for the rest of the week." The blonde woman shrugged fatalistically, as though to say, well, these things happen.

"Oh." Lindsey did not sound surprised. "Do you have an address for her?"

"Let me check. I'm sure there's someone here who has it." She left the lounge where Lindsey was standing and went toward the kitchen at the back of the house. A moment later Lindsey saw Carol's friend, the older nun with short dark hair and intense eyes, look out the kitchen door to see who was asking for Carol.

"Oh, hi," she greeted Lindsey with a friendly smile. "I'm Andrea. Carol went off in a rush this morning. Did you have an appointment with her? Is there something I can help with?"

Lindsey was quiet for a moment, wondering how much this woman knew, what Carol had told her. It was possible she knew everything she and Carol had talked about, and just as possible she knew nothing, that Carol had tried to hide from her what was happening between them.

Finally she drew a deep breath and took the plunge. "I think Carol and I had a misunderstanding last night. I wanted to talk with her about it. Since she's not here, I guess I'll have to write her." She hoped that sounded both matter-of-fact and urgent. She had no idea what the rules about convents were, how willingly this person Andrea would give out Carol's address.

Now it was Andrea's turn to frown. "I'm sorry that happened, Lindsey." She paused. Anyone who looked could see the strain and worry in Lindsey's face. "Sit down a minute. I'll get something to write with. Actually, we just made a fresh pot of coffee. Why don't you take off your raincoat and come have a cup?"

Lindsey nodded, shrugged out of the wet raincoat, and followed Andrea to the kitchen. She was glad to see there was no one else in it. They had all disappeared upstairs or into the various nooks and crannies of this old house.

Lindsey sat down at the kitchen table and thought how when she'd first seen Andrea at the restaurant, her face had seemed stern and foreboding. Today it looked softer. Seeing her like this in the kitchen, wearing old jeans and a sweatshirt, her hair probably not combed yet, just tossed out of her eyes, she wasn't hard or scary at all. Today she looked more like someone who might be Carol's friend.

Andrea set the coffee mugs on the table, found her pen and an old spiral pad, and sat down across from Lindsey. "I thought Carol looked upset last night when she came back from the march. I couldn't tell what it was about. Anyone might have been upset after the emotional strength of that service, and then the violence in the counterdemonstration. So I didn't worry about her too much."

She paused and pushed a piece of paper toward Lindsey with a Springfield address on it. "She's having a hard time. She needs to make some decisions that are going to affect the rest of her life, and she wants to have made them yesterday." She smiled a little sadly, as though she could identify with that. "Carol's strength is not her patience but her ability to assess a situation and make a choice. That works great in law, but sometimes life doesn't cooperate. Sometimes it takes more time to assess life with any accuracy."

Lindsey nodded. "And then, of course, life isn't written down in a book according to chapter, section, and article so you can look it up and know what to do."

"You noticed?" Andrea's amusement was kind.

Lindsey decided to plunge ahead herself and ask the question that had burned in her heart since midnight. "Has she decided not to leave her Community, then? Is that why she went back?"

"Lindsey, I don't know." Andrea answered promptly, brushing her hair back from her face with some impatience. "That is, of course, the burning question she wants to have decided yesterday. Frankly, I think she will leave. I think it will probably be better for Carol and the kind of growing she wants to do. But the process, as you may have noticed, is torture."

She didn't look happy about that, Lindsey thought, watching Andrea's hands play restlessly with the pen and pad. It must be hard for her, too, at some level, to have to watch Carol struggle and come to a different decision than she had herself.

"The important thing," Andrea said abruptly, looking intently at Lindsey now, "is that she make her choice for herself and not because of another person. Do you understand that? That she not leave or stay because of someone she loves? It's too great a burden to put on anyone, on any relationship. I keep telling her that, but I'm not sure she hears me."

Lindsey nodded. "I can understand that. I never thought her choice had anything to do with me."

"I wish Gina did."

Lindsey was confused. What did Gina have to do with anything? Carol had told her a little bit about Gina being back from South America, but it had never sounded like it was very important.

Andrea saw Lindsey didn't understand. "Gina came out here last week to take Carol back to Springfield with her," she explained. "She doesn't want her to leave the Community. Or to leave Gina, I should say. They went back together this morning." She read the shock in Lindsey's face. "I'm sorry," she said gently.

The bicyclist turned this time toward the ocean. She pedaled furiously out Route 6 toward Herring Cove, pedaled as though she wanted to hit the edge running and go spinning into the ocean. Gina. The short woman with dark curly hair holding Carol's hand as they walked away from the ceremony last night. Why hadn't Carol told her? What *had* she told her about Gina?

She threw her bike up against a hedge of wild roses without bothering to lock it and walked vigorously toward the ocean, head down, hands in her pockets under the poncho. The violence of the surf matched the violence of the feelings plunging up and down in her belly. She needed a storm today. She turned and walked along the deserted beach, staying just a few feet from the crashing waves. Was it only a week ago she had sat in the salt spray and let Carol take her hand and lift her out of the surf? Tears streamed down her face, already wet with rain and sea spray.

She tried to find Sheila's voice to calm her plunging thoughts. But she couldn't muster any skepticism. In fact, she couldn't imagine what Sheila would say about this, not if she knew that Lindsey's heart had been deeply engaged in such a short time. She had been drawn to Carol in a new way. It wasn't like the friendship that had grown so slowly between her and Belle, part of the fabric of their everyday life together. And it wasn't the pure lust she had felt that night on the pier with Ra. It was more the sense of possibility. Carol was known and yet unknown, and Lindsey had let herself begin to imagine a future that included Carol, a future that would be new and exciting because it would be different from the present. Lindsey didn't think she had been counting on Carol to rescue her from her own choices about graduate school and the work she wanted to do. No. She wanted to reject that. But it was true that she had felt, particularly in working with Carol on the memorial service, that there were great differences between them, differences in the way they saw the world, and that they could learn from one another, teach one another, grow together in a new and very exciting direction.

Despair washed over Lindsey and fell heavily on her shoulders, bending her knees as she sank down to the sand. Why? Why? What was happening to her? She'd only known this woman a week. Was this really about Carol? They hadn't even been lovers.

The waves continued to swell up toward the beach and break. The gulls drifted in and out of the grey clouds and mist. The sand under her bare legs grew wet and cold after a while, but Lindsey didn't notice. Her thoughts churned on, aimlessly at first, then a little calmer. Finally she could hear some words and phrases that began to make sense to her. They were Andrea's words, she realized, surprised. "You have to make the choices for yourself. You can't choose a life because of another person. It's too great a burden to put on a person or a relationship."

Was that it? Had she been expecting that loving Carol was going to give her some clarity about her own work? The question wasn't really a question. As soon as it became conscious, Lindsey knew that it was true. Carol had been so sure of her work, her direction, how she could help in the world. Being in her religious community or not was a separate issue for Carol. It wasn't about what her work was, more about how she would do it, who she would work with. The work itself, giving legal support to homeless women and children, would stay the same whether she was in a religious community or living on her own—as a lesbian. But now Carol was gone. If it were only that loss, Lindsey thought she could probably deal with it. But it was bigger than Carol's departure: she still had to figure out her life. And there were no easy answers for that one.

Brushing the sand off her legs as she rose, Lindsey drew a deep breath. She wasn't pleased with what she had learned, but this time she was willing to admit that knowing was better than not knowing. She turned back toward the dune where she'd left her bike. She thought she needed to go home and call Sheila.

"If you want happy endings, go to the romance reading." That was Sheila's advice when Lindsey asked her how she could get through the next few hours without committing suicide, getting drunk, or checking herself into the local psych ward. The question was mostly a joke after an hour of talking with Sheila about life, but Sheila's answer was completely serious.

And so it was that Lindsey found herself with Angie and Lisa, wandering back out to the high school on a misty, grey Saturday afternoon. Dozens of other women were going the same direction. Nature couldn't have provided a better audience, Angie observed. Most of these dykes would never have left the beach on a Saturday afternoon if there had been a single ray of sun.

The auditorium was jammed. Angie had gone to Morningstar's reading on Thursday night and there had been a decent turnout, but nothing like this.

"What's the attraction, do you think?" Lindsey mused out loud. "It's not like there's great writing in her books, or even a lot of good sex."

Angie looked at Lindsey as though she had finally been irritated beyond her capacity for forbearance. "Go ahead. Tell me one more time how you all set the standards for what was great literature *and* politically correct in your Women's Studies Program."

Lindsey's face registered astonishment. "*What* are you talking about?"

"You're so critical of everything. What's wrong with reading a book for enjoyment?"

"I *enjoy* books that are well written." Lindsey could tell from Angie's look that she hadn't gotten the point. She looked to Lisa for support. "Lisa, haven't I been Angie's best audience when she's brought those romances out to the beach?"

Lisa shrugged, not willing to be drawn in.

"I do read books that aren't on the great literature list, you know that. I just don't understand why this auditorium is so jammed, that's all I'm saying."

Angie was ignoring her in the quest for seats, leaving Lindsey to ponder the other half of what she'd said. Was she too critical? Lindsey had been raised to believe discrimination was a two-sided word: bad when it was about the misuse of power, good when it was about

selecting among things like TV programs, novels, movies. "Be discriminating," her schoolteacher mother used to tell them. And the
two-edged nature of discrimination had definitely been evident in
women's studies. Male critics dismissed everything women had written as not being worth including in their courses on "great" literature. That was discriminating against women authors. But women
scholars had to discriminate among the books written by women and
find the ones that were truly outstanding. Sure, that meant setting
standards and making judgments, but Lindsey didn't see anything
at all wrong with that. Angie was in a real mood today, and Lindsey didn't know what it was about. Probably Angie's criticism didn't
have anything to do with Lindsey anyhow.

Angie spied three seats in a middle section that weren't being saved,
and they waded through the sea of legs to settle in. Angie stopped
to say hello every three seconds, it seemed to Lindsey, and she and
Lisa had to wait patiently, leaning on chair backs, straddling the knees
of strangers, until Angie was ready to move on. Finally even Lisa lost
patience.

"Angie, let's go claim the seats. You can socialize later." She gave
a small shove from behind, and Angie was instantly obedient.

As Lindsey sank into her seat next to Lisa, she was gradually aware
that she had settled into a sea of white faces in which Lisa stood out
like a dark beacon, announcing. . .what? When Lindsey had gone
places with Belle, it had been like this. At first the feeling of community, of warm congenial social chatter, of being women or dykes
together, alike. And then she would begin to notice, to count the
number of darker faces in the room, if there were any. Lindsey could
feel the alienation creeping up her spine. It wasn't only her bad mood
that left her feeling apart. She glanced sideways to see if she could
tell what Lisa was feeling, but Lisa's face was a cipher.

At first when Lindsey would ask her about it, Belle claimed it didn't
matter, that she herself never noticed. The denial was a survival mech-
anism, no doubt, but it only worked for a short time, giving Belle
the space she needed to assess her situation in this new college environment, in a Women's Studies Department that was great on theory, short on knowing how to follow through and create the world
they were espousing. They were both confused, after a while, because

they knew the women who were trying to live differently, to make a difference; Belle and Lindsey could see their good intentions, knew they cared about Belle. But gradually Belle's very presence seemed to become a reproach, even when she didn't ask the obvious questions: Why am I the only one? Why aren't we offering courses that would attract other women of color? Why is our faculty all white?

Lisa was sitting very quietly beside Lindsey, apparently lost in her own thoughts, as Angie ranged over the auditorium, saying hello to dozens of women and a few gay men hidden in their ranks.

"Lisa?"

"Mmmm?"

"Do you think I'm, well, what Angie says, you know, elitist?"

Lisa turned in her seat to look at Lindsey, a long assessing look that made Lindsey nervous. Lisa was a teacher, a reading teacher. Surely, Lindsey thought, Lisa would agree with her about literature, about Morningstar and the others.

"I don't know about elitist. I think you take a lot on yourself, though."

"What do you mean?"

"I mean, you don't come at life like a learner, you're a fixer. Like you've *got* the answers, not that you're looking for them with the rest of us. I guess it's O.K. I mean sometimes it's nice to think that somebody's got the answers." Lisa softened her words with a laugh. "Right?"

"It sounds pretty obnoxious and dreadful to me." Lindsey felt the criticism and was not mollified. "But is it wrong to know what's racist and sexist and call people on it? Weren't you doing that the other night with Angie and the past lives stuff?"

"Lindsey, don't ask me permission to call people on their racism. You have to decide about that. All I'm saying is you've got to do it from your heart, your gut, from your own experience, not from standing ten feet overhead pointing your finger down at other people. You can't fix problems by saying you got it all figured out and everybody has to do it your way. Shit. That's how we got into this mess in the first place, isn't it?"

Lindsey nodded slowly. She was going to need some time to think about that one. But Angie was coming back to her seat now. Lisa gave her hand a squeeze.

As Lindsey was about to sink into a depressed funk, she saw Margaret Green on the other side of the room with Rachel and Ra's friend Gabrielle. What was Margaret doing here? Lindsey stood up and climbed across a dozen pairs of knees to the aisle.

Threading her way across the room toward the group of older women, Lindsey's loneliness started to resurface. Here were hundreds of women, all of them in couples, she projected. Carol's absence was an ache in her bones, at her very core.

"That was a wonderful poem you read last night," Lindsey said shyly to Margaret. "I couldn't find you afterward, it got so confusing."

"Thanks, Lindsey. I appreciated the conversation that sent me looking for that poem," Margaret offered. "It did get pretty wild there for a minute, didn't it?"

"Is that your roommate over there with you?" Rachel was peering over heads in Angie's direction.

"Angie, you mean? The heavyset woman? Yeah." Lindsey's irritation with Angie was still in her voice. What could Rachel want with Angie?

"I wanted to thank her for bringing the masks to the memorial service last night. It took a lot of courage, I thought, to make a statement like that. Not everyone would have taken the risk."

Lindsey was confused. "What kind of risk?"

"Oh, you know, not a physical risk, but the psychic risk of exposing yourself, or something you believe in and value, exposing it to the world. I thought it was brave."

"They certainly made a striking entrance," Lindsey could agree with Rachel in part. "I thought we were being attacked by a new version of the K.K.K. for a minute when I saw the black robes."

"I know," Rachel laughed. "It did take me a minute to figure out what was happening."

They did a post-mortem on the demo for a few more moments, waiting for the reading to start. As she was turning to go back to her seat Lindsey asked Margaret, almost as an afterthought, "Why are you here? At this event, I mean. Is it part of your job at the Writer's Conference?"

"Goodness, no." Was Margaret laughing at her? "I came because

Beryl is an old friend. And I think her work is unique, important to our community," Margaret added as an afterthought.

Lindsey was surprised. "I don't think I understand what you mean."

"Her books function to create community among lesbians. Sure, they could do more, be more. But look at these women here. They're all affirming the basic premise of Beryl's novels—that lesbians can love one another, and we deserve to have happy, rich, and full lives."

"But what kind of community?" Lindsey was confused. "She never has a Black character in her books, not one who is identified culturally, I mean. Occasionally there's a mention that some woman's skin is darker than another woman's, but it doesn't *mean* anything."

"You're right, of course," Margaret agreed. "She limits the amount of difference she puts into her novels. Mostly she limits it to what a white audience is comfortable with. In real life, white women do that to Black women all the time. Cut them off from their culture, their roots, what it means to be Black." She shrugged. "Beryl Chatham isn't perfect, but I think she can grow if we keep challenging her. She has changed over the years, no doubt about that."

Lindsey pondered Margaret's words as she wound her way back to the seat Angie was saving for her. She wasn't sure someone like Beryl Chatham would grow without being given a very sharp nudge in a productive direction. Margaret, Rachel, Gabrielle. All of those older dykes seemed to know one another. Lindsey fell back on her old explanation when she felt disgruntled, left out: probably Beryl and Margaret had been lovers in college, or something. It didn't seem to help this time. Lindsey was irritated at them all without knowing why.

And then Beryl Chatham came out on the stage. She was a stocky, unprepossessing woman with white hair cut short, but not severe. She seemed dykier to Lindsey than Gabrielle's housewife image, but there was something very familiar and homey about Beryl Chatham, in spite of her romantic name (which she'd made up, Lindsey had heard during her kitchen work days), and in spite of the enthralled groupies, some of whom followed her around the country from reading to reading. There was no flamboyance about this woman, of the kind Aretha Shore cultivated, and it was quite easy for Lindsey to imagine this Beryl Chatham cleaning her own house, feeding her own cat, just like the rest of the world.

"You liked it, didn't you?" Angie's voice was nearly accusatory as they walked toward town after the reading.

"Yeah," Lindsey admitted dreamily. It had given her an hour out of her own life, away from the rampaging thoughts in her head, and for that she was grateful. "I could get into happy endings."

"I guess last night didn't turn out the way you meant it to," Angie said. "I'm sorry if that's what you're upset about." Tears sprang to Lindsey's eyes. She was surprised by Angie's concern, and grateful. "Thanks. I guess it got to me more than I expected." She turned to Angie, remembering what Rachel had said about the masks.

"Angie, why did you decide to bring the masks last night? What was it like for you? Was it scary?"

"Gee, Lindsey, I didn't think you'd even noticed we were there."

Angie's sarcasm was palpable, and Lindsey realized why Angie had been irritated with her earlier in the day. "I guess I've been a little self-absorbed," she apologized to Angie. "Rachel asked me to thank you for bringing the masks when I went over to talk with her before the reading." That wasn't exactly what Rachel had said, but it was close enough. "She said it took a lot of courage for you to do that, you know, bring the masks and dare to say what you think they represent." Lindsey wasn't sure she'd gotten that part right at all, but it seemed to please Angie.

"Really? I thought someone who was a minister would be, well, sort of against what you might call alternative forms of spiritual expression. She thought it was brave, huh?"

Lindsey nodded.

"Maybe I'll have to stop in and talk with her someday. She doesn't sound like your average minister."

Lindsey's first response was defensive. Rachel was her friend, her contact. But then she was glad to see Angie in a better mood. Come to think of it, she was in a much better mood herself. Maybe she could hold on to it through her evening of work.

Lindsey left Angie off at the import store and walked on to Safe Harbor. Walter, the manager, grabbed her as she came through the door. "Thank heavens *you're* here. I was beginning to panic. It's a

Saturday night, you know. You'd think we were coasting into mid-week."

Lindsey looked at Walter like he was crazy. "Walter, I'm only six minutes late for work and I've never missed a night." She tried joking with him a bit. "How come you weren't at Beryl Chatham's reading? Or did I see you in the back with a few of the girls?"

"I don't have time for things like that," he snapped back. "Danny called in. He quit on me. Cold. Just like that. Not a day's notice. You two are such good buddies, I didn't know whether you were in on this or what."

"Danny quit?" Lindsey was stunned. "He never told me. I had no idea. Why did he quit?"

"That's not something he confided in me." Walter seemed a little mollified at Lindsey's distress. Clearly he wasn't facing a conspiracy. "But I don't have anybody in back-up, so you'll be doing extra tables tonight. Everybody will. You'd better get started setting up."

Lindsey was glad she was going to be busy. Carol. Danny. Her whole life in P-town seemed to be disintegrating, falling away from her, and she had no control over it. Beryl Chatham's reading seemed like a calm hour in the center of a storm.

She wished she could re-create the way she felt when the heroine and her lover met in a sunny glade by a rippling stream after a three-year separation. It seemed so right, their coming together. Lots of green imagery and things ripening and rippling, like their love. Their lovemaking was so gentle it was almost sad. Not like the explosion Lindsey had felt that night with Ra's whole hand opening her cunt, Ra's mouth biting hard on her nipple. Stop thinking about that, she commanded her brain as it took off on its own track. Think calm. Think how it didn't matter why they were apart for those years even. They could forgive one another right away and go on. That was because they were each so healthy and centered and doing their own work during that time. They weren't dependent on love or sex for their sanity, for their identity, for their happiness. It was easy, Lindsey was sure while she was listening to Beryl Chatham read, if you could only keep your balance.

Chapter Ten

L indsey worked through the evening, trying to keep her mind focused on balance. Maybe it was the rainy weather, maybe she was getting good at this job finally, or maybe her meditations helped, but the evening was over before she realized it. Without Danny to talk to, she felt like an anonymous, alien soul again, alone among people—the other waiters, Walter—who didn't know who she was. Tonight, not being known was a protection and a comfort. Danny would have asked about Carol, and Lindsey knew she couldn't have talked with him about it yet.

But she was angry at him, too, because she needed to talk with him about the march, examine their planning, discuss what the near-violence of the guys in the trucks and on the motorcycles might mean about how safe they would be the rest of the summer. Several times during the evening she stood with her tab book behind the screen, pretending to add up her checks, listening to the gossip that filtered back to her. Response to the march was pretty intense. Most of the lesbians and gay men were angry at the counterdemonstration, if you could call it that, the harassment. But she heard a few saying there never should have been a march, that it only called attention to us and made us more likely victims. She wondered what Walter thought but was afraid to ask him. She didn't want to hear another tirade about Danny. And she thought Walter might not have approved of the march, he and the other business people. And what was the straight community saying, the folks at the country western bar down by the pier? Did they even know it had happened?

She didn't hear what she needed to hear as she listened—that we were a strong community and had drawn the line. We wouldn't stand silent when one of our own was in danger. She knew she could hear that if she talked to Rachel or Carol or Danny or Ellen. But she wanted to hear it here, stated casually in this public place.

At eleven she walked out of the restaurant, barely remembering her appointment with Sindar. The moon, three-quarters full, was breaking through the last of the clouds, and a drying breeze was coming from the west. The storm front must have moved through, leaving the air unusually warm. Part of her wished it were still raining so that she would have an excuse to go home, hide in her own bed. But it would be a beautiful night for a walk on the dunes. If only her body wasn't so leaden with fatigue. And then she remembered Carol. The grief almost stopped her as she was ready to enter the bar where Sindar was waiting for her, would have stopped her except that she couldn't think what she might better do, where she might better go.

They parked the car Sindar had borrowed in the same spot Lindsey had left her bike that moonless night only a week before. The dunes felt empty and safe to Lindsey tonight, in spite of all her speculations about violence. In some part of her, she still carried the assumption she'd grown up with—she was safe, her neighborhood was safe. Violence was something that happened to people she didn't know.

She and Sindar had spoken very little on the drive out to High Head Beach and walked now in a comfortable silence, Lindsey leading the way toward the ocean. Her heart was beating heavier with the stress of walking in the deep sand, but she still felt calm, like her heart was echoing the steady beat of the drum Sindar had played the night before at the rally.

Lindsey wasn't sure why she was here, wasn't sure why they were here, why being here seemed to be so important to Sindar. She felt she was moving forward as though her body was being pulled along on strings—marionette-style—without her conscious volition. There was a kind of peacefulness, a surrender to the moment, a giving up of responsibility that was rare for Lindsey. She was too tired to even question her lack of control.

Together they crested the rise over the last sand dune before the ocean became visible. Lindsey heard Sindar's breath pull in sharply at the first sight of the moon-white froth on the waves, and she felt Sindar's soft hand in hers as they walked forward, following the path moonlight made on the water.

"Lindsey, it is so beautiful. Thank you for bringing me here." Her hushed voice seemed to credit Lindsey with the creation of what was in front of them. Lindsey ignored a brief impulse to protest.

Sindar appeared overwhelmed by the scene before them; and it was true the ocean and moon were doing their best to create an unforgettable panorama. A single scallop of cloud drifted across the face of the moon, emphasizing the beauty of the night.

"Turn away from the moon for a moment, now, and close your eyes," Lindsey commanded with a sudden energy. It was a game she had played with her brother when they were children on warm summer nights. "Now open them."

And open them they did, to another spectacular sight. The Milky Way stretched in tiny glass glitters across the top of the sky. It had only been concealed from them by the brightness of the moon, but now their eyes could see what was there in front of them.

Finally they turned away and climbed back up in the dunes until Lindsey found a spot in the hard, damp sand very like the one where she had sat and dreamed the week before. Below them the ocean climbed up the shore and then receded, climbed again and fell back, over and over.

Lindsey felt Sindar's breath on her cheek, the cinnamon taste of this woman's lips and tongue probing hers, and she was surprised, but not really. This was not what Lindsey had come here for. And if she wondered about it at all, she would have denied it was the reason Sindar was here either. But for now it was all right, it seemed all right. Or was Lindsey only too tired to protest, to make the effort that would change the direction of what was happening?

They didn't undress, and there seemed to be little urgency in their movements at first, just a gentle rocking of bodies entwined, interlocked in the right way. Sindar had slipped her hard, round thigh between Lindsey's legs, brought it right up against the rough seam of her pants crotch, and began to move up and down, up and down. Mesmerized, Lindsey lay quietly at first, one hand holding Sindar's shoulder as she rocked, the other resting on the back of her head, feeling the tightly braided dreads, pressing Sindar's mouth tight to her own.

She had never made love with someone she felt no physical or emotional attraction to, never wanted sex because her body wanted physical comfort, and then sought out someone—anyone—to fill the need. She could joke with Danny about such things, but part of the joke was that she could not imagine herself doing something she would consider so irrational, so uncaring. And yet, now, she did not feel uncaring, only slightly detached from herself as she let her lips explore Sindar's lips, cheek, ear, and then mouth again.

Her hands found Sindar's flesh under her shirt, and she marveled at how firm her large breasts were. Her fingers slid off the taut mounds, sought the warmth of the fold of flesh between breast and belly, then moved back up to Sindar's prominent nipples. She wanted to slide her mouth down and circle those nipples with her lips, but the rhythm of their movement had its own momentum. And just for a moment, Lindsey felt shy. She hadn't meant to be making love to Sindar tonight.

She couldn't take the lead, that would require too much effort. Giving herself to Sindar's lead seemed easier, somehow. Or perhaps it was a different way of claiming herself, claiming the desire that started to rise in her belly, her thighs, in spite of the questions her mind was churning out.

Then Sindar pushed her thigh harder against Lindsey's cunt. Lindsey felt her hands reach down and grab Sindar's ass cheeks, pulling her tight. All of a sudden she understood with her body what her head had been rejecting. She needed this, needed to be touched, to be pulled out of herself. Her body responded, almost violently, as she matched Sindar's rhythm. Together they rocked, feeling the tension build, the wetness seep through cloth. "Oh, yes," one of them moaned softly, and it could have been either.

Lindsey felt Sindar's orgasm begin when her rhythm changed, became more urgent, forceful, and her faster thrusts brought Lindsey over the edge too, let her gasp with relief as she felt the orgasm ripple up her thighs and into her belly.

For a while they held each other without words. "That was nice,"

Lindsey said finally, her sense of etiquette overcoming her desire to not break the spell.

"Yes," Sindar agreed. "I was feeling lonely. Thank you for being here with me." Then she was quiet again.

Lindsey looked at her with surprise. Sindar, lonely? Even though she was here with Evelyn and Gloria? But maybe they were lovers. Maybe Sindar had a lover at home. Maybe she didn't. Lindsey realized she knew nothing about the small round woman she was holding in her arms, nothing at all. Everything she thought she knew about Sindar was an assumption, and now she couldn't remember what her assumptions had been based on, what need of her own she might have been fulfilling by imagining Sindar.

Her train of thought was gathering speed when suddenly it was derailed. Sindar was unbuttoning Lindsey's blouse, letting her fingers tickle the valley between her breasts, pausing to kiss Lindsey's shoulders as the blouse fell away. Lindsey felt shy again, unable to banter with Sindar as she had with Ra. What in the world was wrong with her? She'd just made love with this woman, why was she so numb now?

Sindar felt her hesitation. "Is this all right?" Her hands rested lightly on Lindsey's shoulders.

"Yes. No. I . . ." Lindsey was at a loss for words. How could she say what was wrong when she didn't know herself? "I'm a little tired, Sindar." She groaned inwardly at how that must sound. Why not just say she had a headache or some other cliché-ridden shit? Or the sand was too wet and had soaked through her jeans? But she was tired, and the sigh that escaped her weighted-down chest was real, and so were the tears that Sindar couldn't see but found with her lips.

Sindar was still for a moment, then gently slid Lindsey's blouse back over her shoulders and kissed her cheek.

"Let's just sit for a while?" Lindsey asked it as a question. She couldn't have moved. Her bones and muscles seemed to have softened, and for a fleeting moment she wondered if she would melt right into the sand as the rain had seeped through earlier in the evening.

They sat until the moon had passed far over their heads and the night breeze became too cool. They walked back in silence, hands linked lightly together, but Lindsey felt burdened by the silence she could not break.

Sindar gave Lindsey a long hug when she pulled up in front of the house to let Lindsey out. She looked deep into Lindsey's eyes. It was all Lindsey could do not to turn away.

"We will talk tomorrow, Lindsey." Her voice sounded almost normal, Lindsey thought, not like a woman who was angry or upset, not like a woman who had been counting on someone who didn't come through.

Lindsey nodded, then found her voice. "Good night, Sindar. I'm glad we could walk on the dunes."

"Yes. It was very beautiful. Good night, Lindsey."

My dreams that night were wild. It sure was crowded in my head. In one short segment of an early dream, I heard the voice of my fourth-grade health teacher repeating piously that our bodies were temples of God and we had to keep them clean and pure. I mean, really! So I hadn't taken a shower before I fell into bed and could still smell Sindar's scent on my hands and hair. Did I deserve Mrs. Simpson's voice half an hour later? In other parts of the dream, Carol kept leaving. I'd catch a glimpse of her back as she walked away from me, sometimes like at the march, once like after our breakfast date when she'd waved good-bye and smiled, but mostly she was leaving me in places we hadn't even been together yet. I wasn't too happy about that as a prediction of my future.

But mainly, it was about Belle. Yeah. It surprised me, and then I thought, why was it a surprise? It was Belle throwing her arms around me when we made love and sobbing, "Don't leave me, don't ever leave me," and then she was gone. It was Belle, her face close up to mine, telling me how much she depended on me to get her through something, and then she was gone. And it was me, thinking I could be everything she wanted and feeling like a personal failure when it turned out I wasn't what she wanted.

I gave up the pretext of sleep pretty early and took my bike out to Race Point. I wanted a nice long expanse of beach, a good wind to blow the dust out of my brains, and no company. I hoped it wouldn't become a habit, this having traumas and heading for the beach. Two mornings in a row was taking its toll.

Exercise helped, but I couldn't make sense of it by myself. What did Sindar have to do with all those images of Belle and Carol walking away from me? I mean, I'm not stupid. I got that Sindar and Belle were both Black, and I got that one of the themes was abandonment. But beyond that I couldn't go. And I'd had my weekly long-distance call with Sheila after yesterday's trauma. If I called again, she'd tell me to come home. It wasn't worth the effort. No. I was kidding myself. Those were my words. Sheila's voice would never say quit trying to understand. Maybe I needed to listen to myself this time. Maybe I just needed to live it, instead of figuring out what it all meant so I could have the correct response.

I biked back to the house for a late breakfast and walked in on Lisa and Sindar having a cup of coffee. Had Sindar come to see me? Did she want—? And then I did it. All by myself I stopped the questions and poured a cup of coffee.

Lisa was listening intently as Sindar described growing up in Trinidad. I put a bagel in the toaster.

Lisa waved me over to join them at the table. I felt a little shy, as well as fearful, but Sindar nodded and smiled. She seemed a little shy too.

"I was telling Lisa about my grandmother's house."

"Yeah. I heard a little. Was it hard, living so far away from everything?"

"For many years it was wonderful. I think I did not miss what I did not know I could have. My playmates were the sand crabs and the sea birds."

Lisa was frowning. "Are you saying you didn't know you were poor?"

"No. Not exactly. I knew my father had gone to the United States to pick fruit, and we waited for his money to come. When it stopped coming, my mother had to go. I didn't know for many years that there were people who didn't have to live like we lived. I knew we were poor, but I did not understand that others were rich."

"Wow. I mean, all I had to do was look around me and see the big cars driving past our neighborhood on the way to the suburbs, or watch TV, or read a newspaper." Lisa seemed surprised that Sindar's experience was so different from hers.

Sindar nodded. "As soon as I went to the village, I understood. Maybe my grandmother told me before then. But as a six- or seven-year old I was more interested in the life around me, the life I could see."

I put more butter on my bagel and tried not to feel guilty or depressed as I thought about my own middle-class childhood home.

Sindar went on to tell us how her grandmother had raised her, then pushed her out of the house to go to elementary school every day, and finally encouraged her to go into town and live in the girls' boarding school.

Lisa was nodding thoughtfully as if this was more familiar ground. I'd heard her say that learning to read was her way into a new life, first because she could imagine living differently, and then because reading was a skill, the first skill, really, that made other learning possible. Lisa was passionate about her fourth graders learning to read, to *love* reading.

"I met Gloria and Evelyn at boarding school," Sindar continued. "They were a couple of years older and took me on as a younger sister." Sindar said her mother lived in Canada now, worked as a maid in Toronto.

As I listened to Sindar talk about her life, I heard her saying she had been a solitary child, finding comfort in nature. I had been a child in a large family, going to nature for solitude and escape. Had those two worlds come together for a moment last night on the dunes?

When Lisa dashed off to work, Sindar and I sat on. The silent barrier between us seemed to have fallen away. As long as we talked about our childhoods. It was fun to see how alike we were in some ways, in spite of our differences. The imaginary games we played with the animals around us, the dreamy hours spent alone staring at a moving stream—those we shared. And for me it was the first time I'd ever let anyone know that part of me, the first time I'd thought it important enough to share.

Later I remembered what Margaret Green had said about Beryl Chatham's novels—how she only put in as much difference as a white audience could tolerate—and I wished we had talked more about how different we were, how different were the needs that took us out on the dunes.

I couldn't let the subject of last night alone, although I wanted to, and even though it seemed that Sindar was perfectly comfortable with both last night and today.

"I'm sorry about last night, Sindar." Maybe she would say she understood, even though I didn't, and it would be over. But no.

"What are you sorry about, Lindsey?" She didn't look hurt or defensive, just curious.

"That I...ummm...that I couldn't...that I was too tired." I stopped in frustration. What *was* I sorry about?

"You are sorry for being tired? We all work very hard. It is normal to be tired." She paused. "Do you mean you are sorry we walked together on the dunes? Or that we kissed? Or that we gave each other pleasure?" Her voice wasn't angry. At least it didn't sound annoyed to me. It gave me permission to see what I did mean.

"No. I'm not sorry about any of those things. I guess I mean I just can't take it further." That was it. I knew it when I said it. I couldn't be lovers with Sindar right now, not when I was still so focused on Carol.

"Oh." She looked relieved, smiled at me sunnily. "I was afraid you were saying you had done something you didn't want to do. Tomorrow is not a problem, Lindsey. We are going on with our tour tomorrow. To Boston. Then Portland and Nova Scotia."

Of course. How could I have been so stupid? What did I think, that she would throw her arms around me like I was an anchor in the storm-tossed sea and beg me never to leave her?

"I was lonely." There, she'd said it again. "And a little nervous and afraid." She didn't look ashamed of that. "It is our first tour. Not all of our audiences will be like here in Provincetown."

I was nodding, relaxing a little. It seemed that nothing more was required of me, which gave me the space to think about her.

"Will you see your mother, do you think? In Canada?"

"I hope so. I have not seen her for eight years. That is one thing I am nervous about. She knows nothing about my life today."

We talked on as our coffee got cold and the lunch hour came and went. I liked learning to know Sindar, and it did not escape me that she was very little like the Sindar I would have described only yesterday.

I was sorry when it was time for me to go to work. Sindar and I hugged again. I gave her my address at school in case the group came back down through New England in the fall. I felt like I might have a new friend, but some part of me was afraid I didn't deserve her.

I don't know exactly how I got through the next two weeks. I'd like to have turned my mind off and coasted, but as you may have noticed, my brain doesn't work that way. Exercise helped. I started running again, nearly every day before I went out to Herring Cove for my couple of hours on the beach. If I ran, then rode my bike out to the beach, then worked extra tables at the restaurant, usually I could fall asleep at night without too much background noise about what I might have done differently with Carol, or what did that night on the beach with Sindar mean, anyway, or why was I avoiding Ra so carefully.

Things at our house quieted down, too. Angie and Lisa seemed to have found a way to talk without snarling or referring to past lives. They'd known one another since second grade at Framingham Central School, so it couldn't have been the first time they'd needed to work this sort of thing out. Ellen was a little less hyper now that *Torch Song* was settling into a long run. There was even talk of taking this production into Boston for a couple of weeks at the end of the summer.

I was beginning to like this house I'd stumbled into by accident, on a tip from a friend of Sheila's who knew someone in Boston who had just told her about a space in a dyke house in P-town.

So July moved on. I seemed to be surviving without Carol, though the ache of sexual longing that had been with me during that week of wonderful anticipation settled into a duller ache of loneliness. I wrote to her right away, a brief note explaining Sindar's assumption that night. There was a lot I could have said, and a lot I didn't say, but none of it seemed relevant if she was really going to stay with her Community. And with Gina. I just didn't want her to think I had been about to abandon her the night of the march, after the promises we had made—silent promises, but to me they were promises nonetheless—standing with our hands linked, lighting our candles.

I missed Danny a lot. After the experience with Sindar, I felt like I was ready to take the discussion about masks one step further, but I didn't think I could do it by myself. Something was going around in my head about how the masks give us space behind them, space we need to shift and practice and grow. And it seemed to me that if we sometimes deliberately let someone think we are different than we really are, it is because we need to practice being different until it becomes the new us. Why am I using *we?* I mean *me*. Sindar thought what happened on the beach was great. We each gave, we each got. No promises, no need for me to be perfect—or even not tired. To her, I was O.K.; I was practicing being O.K. with me.

I wasn't any closer to figuring out my life, but I was getting more comfortable with it. I talked with Sheila once a week—to keep grounded, kind of. I was pretty clear I'd go back to graduate school in the fall. Not because anything about the M.S.W. program had changed, but because I suspected I was changing and I wanted to see what might happen.

And Angie kept reminding us all that the summer wasn't over, we still had the best part to come. She talked so much about how great August was that I started to believe it. I woke up one morning and imagined I heard Ed McMahon's voice rolling out, "And here'sssssss August."

Chapter Eleven

It was the first week in August when Angie came home one night and said she'd seen Danny at one of the bars late the night before. It was one of the local hangouts, not a gay bar. Angie said it was a pretty rough place with a lot of drugs. That made me sad. I didn't know for sure he was drinking and drugging again, but if he'd hung around P-town and wasn't in touch with me or his old AA friends, the news wasn't good.

I waited a couple of nights, hoping I'd see Danny on the street during the day, something normal where we could talk like nothing had happened. But finally after work one night I went down to the tavern at the outer edge of town. Murphy's Bar and Grill it said in green neon. I could hardly get in the front door for the motorcycles parked on the sidewalk.

Danny was there, sitting at a table with some other guys you would never mistake for faggots. And Danny had changed too. His pigtail was gone and his crewcut had grown out an inch or so. A glass with something dark in it was sitting in front of him. It could have been a Coke, or dark beer, or some kind of mixed drink. He must have seen me come in the door because he was at my side in a second.

"Lindsey, what are you doing here? You don't belong here. Go on back over to Commercial Street." His voice was harsh, and he spoke so fast his words seemed stuck together. Maybe he just wasn't articulating too clearly.

"You don't belong here either, Danny." What the hell? I wasn't going to waste time on pleasantries if he wasn't. "I want to talk with you."

"Not here." One hand on my elbow, he was propelling me toward the door I'd just come through.

"Where?" I was firm, stood planted in the entrance.

"I'll meet you at the Sunshine Cafe tomorrow at ten. Just go now."

"O.K. But if you don't come, Danny, I'll be back here tomorrow night and I won't be easy to get rid of."

"I'll come." His voice was husky now, and for a moment I thought he was going to cry. But he didn't. He nodded, then turned his back on me and returned to the table.

I wheeled my bike through an alley next to the bar, taking a short cut back to Commercial Street. Parked in the alley was a truck I was getting to know pretty well by now, black and chrome with a bank of spotlights across the top of the cab. Why was I not surprised? Depressed, I headed home.

Danny wasn't just there the next morning, he was there ahead of me. Sitting in a booth with a cup of coffee in front of him, sunbeams slanting across the length of the room, it was easier to see him as the Danny I'd known. Except for the strain in his eyes. And the way he wouldn't look at me straight on at first.

"So?" I sat down and opened the conversation. No beating around the bush.

He shrugged. "It happens. It happens a lot." He meant people start using again. "Maybe I just couldn't get away from the stuff."

I looked at him closely, was sure he was lying. I didn't know *why* he was lying, but it made me glad. "You're not using again, Danny. Cut the crap." I took a sip of my coffee and eyed him carefully, the way he usually watched me. "So what's the deal? What's happening? Where's Jose Alfredo?" For I knew in my bones he was connected with this somehow, and he'd disappeared about the same time as Danny.

Danny winced at Jose Alfredo's name. Shrugged again. "Gone. You know, it happens to me all the time." He was trying to laugh.

"Oh, Danny, I'm sorry. This one was supposed to be different. You said this one was different."

"Yeah, well, I was wrong." He looked down at his hands gripping the coffee mug, and I knew he was lying again. How did I know that? I'm not sure, but I was willing to bet that Jose Alfredo hadn't just gone off with another lover. There was more to this than Danny wanted me to know. The answer came to me in the proverbial flash, and I said it out loud before I could deny it to myself.

"You're selling, aren't you, Danny?"

But Danny had his mask firmly in place. He didn't even flinch. Just shrugged and took another sip of coffee.

"Let's talk about you. How are you doing? Did you ever make it with the nun?"

I wasn't depressed now, I was scared. Ever since the night of our march, the gossip was that the gay man who was murdered had been running drugs, or that it was a failed drug connection, but definitely we were hearing it was drug-related.

When I didn't answer, Danny looked at me finally and saw I was scared.

"Leave it alone, Lindsey. I'm O.K. In a couple of weeks I'll be back at Harvard, grinding out the papers and case studies for the old M.B.A. I just had a couple of things to do first. Don't worry about it, O.K.?" He grinned, and for a minute I was sitting with the old Danny, the Danny whose spirit I knew pretty well, since it matched mine in some important ways.

What could I say? I told him a little bit about Carol. He knew right away how hard it was for me that she'd left like that. He'd seen me jumping in with both feet before I bothered to test the water. "You taking care of yourself?" he wanted to know. That was just like Danny. I trot out here to rescue him and he's making sure I'm all right.

He asked how things were at Safe Harbor. I didn't have a lot of gossip. Since I'd gone back to being an anonymous person, nobody did what Danny had been willing to do—force me out, challenge my act, make me share myself.

Then it was over and we were out in the sun and Danny was smiling, looking almost like himself, waving at me, saying, "Hasta la vista, Lindsey," like we were going to see each other every other morning.

"Hasta luego," I muttered unhappily. Later. Much later.

I pulled myself together and headed out to the beach. Let the sun burn this irritation away. Let the shock of cold water numb the throb growing just behind my forehead.

The crowd of dykes swarming to Herring Cove had grown bigger and bigger every day as August neared. August was prime dyke time, Angie told me. It may have looked like there were a lot of us in June or July, but just wait, she promised, just wait until August.

Today it was August for real. A line of women sat with their beach chairs facing the sun *and* the entrance from the parking lot. I walked by, feeling at first like I did sometimes when I passed a construction crew working on the street. Then I started to get into it and slowed down a little, letting the sand tug my feet as I checked out the dyke parade review. All sizes and shapes and colors. There must have been twenty of them, looking at me as hard as I was looking at them. "Look's like your type, Dede," somebody hollered. "Nice legs," shouted somebody else, and I couldn't help grinning. I liked theirs, too. All of them. Seeing Danny had put me back in the mood to be human.

Ellen and Lisa were in our usual spot—not too far up in the dunes, but far enough away from the waves so we would not be overwhelmed by high tide. I settled in for a nap, wanting the throb in my head to be gone when I woke up. But Lisa and Ellen were dissecting their friend Angie. Good-bye nap.

"You know who she's dating, don't you, Lisa?" Ellen's voice was accusatory. "Why is it such a big secret?"

"Angie likes her privacy," Lisa said, not admitting anything. "There's nothing wrong with that. I may have my suspicions, but it's hers to tell, isn't it?"

"Privacy. Yuck. That isn't really possible in our house," I protested. "And what do you mean *dating?* Isn't that something hets do before they get into high school?"

"No, I think the concept of dating has entered the gay and lesbian world, too." Ellen was quite serious, I saw with more than a little surprise. "It's when you're definitely sexually attracted to someone and if you were teenagers you'd have just gone to bed on the first date but when we're older we date once or twice to try and figure out whether we'll be devastated by going to bed with this one or whether it will be O.K. if we act on this sexual attraction." She ended and took a deep breath to replenish what she'd lost with that mouthful.

"I confess, I never thought of it quite that way," I told her. "So is Angie dating someone? I thought she was just having an affair. I mean, she spends some nights away. You don't do that if you're dating, do you?" I was asking Ellen for clarification.

"You might. It depends on how nervous you are."

"Oh. I see," I said, not seeing at all.

I went down for my first dip of the day then. I always try to force myself into the water early during my two hours at the beach so that the next couple of times won't be so hard. If I lie there and sweat for a long time, the water seems to get colder and colder as I get hotter and hotter. Today it wasn't bad. I dove in and stretched my arms and legs in a breaststroke that let me ride the waves and see what was happening all around me.

What I saw was Ra. Coming down to the water. I could tell that she'd seen me, too, and we were going to talk. Oh, well. Maybe it was time. I'd pleaded too busy the last couple of Friday nights when she'd been in the restaurant. But here she was swimming right out to me. Hard to look busy when you're floating on your back to the rhythm of the waves.

"Did you reach your edge?" she asked after we swam and joked a while, then went up to the beach to sit and rest.

"I don't know what you mean."

"It seemed like you were interested in exploring some things—and then you stopped being interested. We all have an edge it's hard to go past. I just wondered if you'd reached yours, or if it was something else." She wasn't chastising me, she was just interested.

"I did get distracted, focused on someone specific. I think that's the only reason." I wasn't sure that was true, but then I still didn't know exactly what edge Ra was talking about. "She's gone now," I said, and was surprised at how sad it sounded.

Ra was quiet for a moment. Then, "I'm sorry," she said.

I seem to have heard that a lot lately. I just nodded, unwilling to discuss Carol with her.

"You have a wonderful capacity for being open, vulnerable, Lindsey. It's exciting to me, you know that." She was smiling at me now, a friendly kind of smile, almost casual as she said these things that seemed not at all casual to me.

"I wondered if, maybe, you'd like to explore another part of yourself?" She offered that just as casually, leaning back on her elbows and letting her legs fall open, her thighs be touched by sun.

What was I going to say? "Sorry, no I don't think so?" Or, "I prefer not knowing myself?" That one might be true, but I would never admit it out loud.

I confess, I was curious. What *was* it about Ra that so excited me? I could feel my cunt start to tingle with the memory of her fingers and tongue, and we hadn't even started talking dirty. At least, I didn't think we had.

I took a deep breath. I may not have known what edge she was talking about, but I jumped off it. "Tell me what you mean," I said.

When I went back up on the beach to Ellen and Lisa, they were still working on Angie's sex life, but that seemed a hundred years away to me. What had I agreed to? Was I really up to this, or was Ra right? I knew if I hadn't actually reached my edge, I was very close to it. I didn't have to go tonight. She'd said that a couple of times. That she'd be there, but I didn't have to go.

I biked home for my shower, stood under the hot stinging water, biked to work, began setting up my tables, all without coming out of the fierce concentration Ra had left me in. This wasn't at all like the feelings I'd had about Carol. Right? My heart was beating heavily, I could feel the pulse in my neck, my scalp was even tingling. Surely this was anticipation, just like I'd anticipated being with Carol, making love to her.

Ra said she would be waiting for me when I finished work. She would be waiting, she would be completely passive, waiting for me to decide what to do. She would be alone in her room. She would be naked on her bed. The door would be unlocked. I could come when I was ready. Or I could decide not to come.

My hands were shaking as I set the tables. What was so different about this, anyway? Sometimes I'd made love to Belle and she'd been too tired to make love back to me. What did it matter that Ra had said in advance what we would do? Did saying it out loud make it seem more dangerous, forbidden? Maybe I wouldn't go after all. Maybe I would just bike home and fix some popcorn and hang out.

Sitting at the beach this afternoon, I'd asked Ra why she liked this way of pushing against edges, as she called them.

"I was born and grew up in South Boston," she said. "Poor. Czechoslovak. Catholic. Gretchen Razinski. My boundaries were very specific and very limited. I knew I'd have to push against them to survive. But my ties and responsibilities to that place, to my people, those were pretty strong too. I still live in the neighborhood I was born in. I teach school in the school I went to as a child. So I had to find other ways to stretch, other boundaries I could break. Moving to California wasn't going to do it for me."

I found myself listening very closely. There was not a lot I could identify with. My world had never seemed closed in. I was always being told that limitations were in my imagination: they weren't real, and I shouldn't let them stop me. I had moved to the East Coast, but it could have been the West Coast, my family never would have done anything but encourage me.

"I had to learn there were different ways to be active, to be powerful," Ra was saying. "And that some things that looked passive weren't necessarily bad. You know how to take pleasure. You may have thought of yourself as passive when I made love to you out on the pier that night, but you were receiving, actively receiving. I need to know more about that. My tendency is to control things too much, and sometimes I hurt other people by not letting them give me what they want to give me."

"And you, Lindsey," Ra's voice went on in my memory, "you need to learn more about taking control, about being active."

I'd protested at that point. I certainly never thought of myself as a wallflower, as somebody who let other people do things. Ra was ready for me. "I'm not saying there is anything wrong with you, anything wrong about how you are in the world. I'm inviting you to learn more about another way of being in the world. You don't have to use power once you understand it. But you can't use it at all if you don't know how."

By the time my first customers had filed through the restaurant, I was convinced I didn't want this knowledge. There was something wrong with the way Ra talked about this stuff. It was too neat. Power was messy, certainly power the way it was used in the world. What I wanted wasn't power over someone, but mutuality and love.

Ra's voice was there waiting for me. "It isn't about power over another person, Lindsey. It's about understanding your relationship to power." And then she'd started describing what we could do, what

I could do. By the third round of customers, I was remembering how her thighs looked open in the sun, and I was starting to imagine what it would be like to touch her wherever I wanted, as slowly or deeply as I wanted.

"I'm outta here," I told Walter at 10:45, and stood in front of the restaurant for a moment, inhaling the damp sea air. It was a noisy, unsettled Saturday night, more boisterous than some, I thought, as I watched the crowd lining up down the street to get into a disco. To go or not to go, that was the question, and I had about made up my mind to end the suspense and head home when someone called my name.

"Lindsey, hey Lindsey." It was Danny. I crossed the street to the doorframe he was standing inside, leaning casually in the shadow. "You're done early. No business tonight?"

For some reason I was angry at him, standing there just like things were normal between us, like he hadn't gone off to do goddess knows whatever awful things. "No, Danny, I've got a date. I'll see you later, O.K.?" It wasn't really a question. I was turning to walk down toward Ra's guesthouse.

"I'm catching the last bus out to Boston," he said, as I turned away. "I'm done here. I wanted to say good-bye and . . ." He paused and put his hand in his pocket. "If anything comes up, call this number, will you?"

God, was I irritated with him. He could have said good-bye this morning, or let me know he was going to lead a normal life again. I shoved the piece of paper in my pocket. "Sure, Danny. Hope it goes well," I said in a hurry, and walked away leaving him hunched in the corner of the doorway.

Without really having to choose, I was walking toward Ra's.

There are moments in life that you replay later, over and over, wishing you could fix them, wishing you could time travel back to the few minutes preceding and then take a different course. Usually it isn't about a huge wrenching change, it's just a slight shift, a yes instead of a no, or vice versa, walking down this block instead of that; and then the strands of time could weave together again and everyone would basically be the same except for this one thing would be fixed.

Walking toward Ra's, Lindsey wasn't thinking about strands of time. That would come later. She was trying to keep her feet headed in the same direction they'd started, one in front of the other. She was trying to keep her mind blank so that she didn't panic. This was the ultimate test, in some way, of Sheila's urging that she just act, not plan out every minute, imagine every consequence. Because if she started imagining what she would find, she wouldn't go. And something in Lindsey was compelled toward this learning. For reasons she didn't understand, the compelling was stronger right now than the fear that, at other times, would have sent her running in the opposite direction down Commercial Street.

She stood outside the neatly painted little white guesthouse to catch her breath, then mounted the stairs slowly. "You can take your time," Ra had told her when she described the evening to Lindsey, "you can do everything at your own speed."

She hoped she would not meet anyone in the foyer. She couldn't climb those stairs if Joan or Gabrielle were in the living room, watching, knowing what was happening. But the dimly lit parlor was empty. A rocking chair in front of an open window rocked slightly, silently.

She walked down the long hall toward the door at the end, Ra's room. She had no doubt that Ra was there, just as she had promised, lying on the bed—naked, vulnerable, waiting. The carpet cushioned her footsteps, but she was sure Ra would know she was there, standing outside this door, deciding whether or not to come in.

She turned the knob and stepped into the room. It was familiar to her. She remembered the wedgewood blue woodwork that seemed to absorb rather than reflect the soft candlelight. And lying naked on the bed, arms over her head, thighs open, was Ra. Gretchen Razinski.

Lindsey walked over to the edge of the bed and looked down. She could tell that Ra was watching her but could not really make eye contact in the dark shadows of candlelight. And then—Lindsey's breath caught sharply as she saw the rest. Looking more closely, she could see that Ra's wrists were bound to the bedstead over her head, bound by soft pieces of cloth, it seemed, twisted together. Lindsey reached down and touched the ropes, then ran her finger down Ra's arm, around the bottom of her breast, and up to her nipple.

She had been ready to stay until she saw the ropes. What did they mean? They were soft, loose. They didn't really bind Ra. But she was shaken. They were a statement, a statement that made Lindsey uncomfortable. Then she remembered what Ra had said. "You'll be totally in charge. It will be up to you. You can do whatever you want."

She stepped back from the bed and took her clothes off, threw them on the chair. Then she went up and stood again by the bed. She leaned over and untied the ropes and tossed them lightly over toward her clothes. She began to talk to Ra.

"Turn over," she commanded, her voice calm and firm. Ra did.

She remembered how Ra had told her what she was going to do that night on the pier, how Lindsey's mind had become part of the sex play, anticipating each touch. Her body had responded often before Ra even touched her.

She told Ra she was not allowed to move her arms, to use her hands, that Lindsey would be the only one moving. She told Ra she could not have an orgasm until Lindsey told her it was all right. Ra should remember that. It might seem easy now, but later it would be harder. It would be harder as Lindsey's hands stroked up Ra's legs, gently massaging as she touched higher and higher, pushing the muscles in an upward motion as she stroked toward Ra's ass, the cheeks standing out in stark relief, white against Ra's dark suntan across her legs and lower back.

In the dark, known only to herself, Lindsey's face began to flush with excitement as she watched Ra's back tense, then relax as Lindsey's fingers reached toward her cunt, then moved away.

Suddenly Lindsey's hands stopped. "Open your legs for me," she commanded. Ra hesitated, then her knees opened. Lindsey knelt in the space between Ra's legs, looking at this woman, prone beneath her, waiting for her touch, and felt an excitement different from what she had ever known. Without touching Ra's legs, Lindsey slid her fingers into the slippery, wet vagina.

"Remember," she said softly, "you aren't allowed to have an orgasm until I say it's time." She put the palm of one hand flat on Ra's ass and pushed up, making the dark opening more available, and began to run her finger around and around the edge of Ra's vagina.

She felt the woman's whole body shudder and breathe in deeply. Could Ra have an orgasm differently, Lindsey wondered, could she make Ra come without following Ra's so precise direction?

For another hour, perhaps—it felt like years had passed—Lindsey played with Ra's body. She made her turn over again, lie with her breasts exposed. She began her light touches at the tip of Ra's fingers, up over her head, and moved down her strong arms to her breasts. Lindsey's fingers circled Ra's nipples, never quite touching, then went down to her navel. She smiled as Ra began to moan. Her own excitement mounted. Straddling Ra's waist, she put her fingers in her own cunt. God, she was wet, she didn't think she'd ever been this wet. Ra's eyes were wide, watching Lindsey.

"You'd like me to be doing this to you, wouldn't you?" Lindsey understood, too, that Ra would like to be in Lindsey's place, in charge, moving her fingers in and out of Lindsey's cunt. Her orgasm was quick, fierce and sweet. It gave her energy she hadn't known she possessed. "You'd like to have an orgasm like that, wouldn't you?" she said to Ra. "But you have to wait."

She moved further down on the bed and spread Ra's legs again, leaned forward and put her mouth on the wet tangle of pubic hair. Ra's moans became rhythmic as Lindsey's tongue probed deeper and deeper. She wanted to swallow this whole cunt, suck the juice out and swallow it. Gradually she let her tongue move up toward Ra's clitoris, never resting there, never pushing hard, just flicking past the hard little button. She wanted Ra to feel the edge and move away from it, feel it approach, near, nearly go over, and then have to stay still while it receded again. She told Ra what she was doing and heard her groan of recognition. Lindsey felt strength in her body, her hands, her mouth and tongue. The night could be passing, turning to dawn, but she still had energy, and Ra—she felt it—Ra still had desire.

Finally, when her own passion had built again and was about to wash over her in another orgasm, Lindsey leaned forward and whispered to Ra, "I release you. Take what you need." She felt Ra's arms lock around her, their legs intertwine as Ra thrust up against Lindsey's thigh. Lindsey rode her like that, moving back and forth, back and forth, a frenzy welling up from deep in her core. She came once, and Ra was still moving, still gasping, holding Lindsey's buttocks tight against her. Lindsey came again, the orgasm never releasing, but building back up as Ra kept thrusting. She felt Ra's body shudder just as she was coming again and knew they were finished, knew they were climbing back down from the edge, but climbing down it now from the other side, having slid over into the dark place that was no longer so unknown.

Chapter Twelve

Danny waited in the shadow of the doorway while Lindsey swung down the street and out of sight. Then he shrugged slightly, an accepting rather than dismissing shrug. Had he a right to expect more from Lindsey after consciously distancing himself from her for weeks? His shrug said, no, said this is the consequence I expected. He looked at his watch, hitched his jeans up, and walked quickly down the alley next to Safe Harbor leading to the private dock behind the restaurant. His empty backpack hung slackly from his shoulder.

When he came back out of the alley, it was after eleven-thirty. He walked quickly toward the center of town. Anyone seeing him would have thought he was another vacationer, run out of time, heading for the midnight bus back to the mainland, all of his belongings in the full daypack he wore on his back. At ten minutes before midnight he went into the men's room on the dock next to the bus that was loading. He came out as the last passengers were loading, the driver slamming the luggage compartments closed, and walked toward the bus. The black truck with dark windows sat just ahead of the bus, its engine idling softly.

The bus driver saw the kid—looked about twenty years old—start to get on the bus. Then a buddy of his came and slapped him on the back, took his arm. Said something about a party. The kid didn't look too happy, but he went with him. Hell, you know how these kids are. Plan to do one thing one minute, off doing another the next. The bus driver figured he'd changed his mind. No reason he couldn't go to Boston the next day.

There was quite a party that night, not in Provincetown, but out a ways. Families camping up at Head of the Meadow Beach heard the cars and trucks roaring past after midnight. The beach is closed at dark, but there are no barricades, no way to keep people out when they want to party on a Saturday night. A squad car swings past now and then, but North Truro doesn't have much need for heavy patrolling. It was after 3:00 A.M. when the campsite staff reported hearing shots down on the beach, and someone finally called the police. The moon was setting by then, and a breeze whispered through the pines over the tents. The campers who'd been awakened by the noise turned over and went back to sleep.

Lindsey was in a deep, sound sleep herself on Sunday morning when Angie came crashing into the bedroom, dumped the newspapers on the floor, sat heavily on Lindsey's bed, and started sobbing. Lindsey struggled out of sleep, muttering with irritation. When she realized it was Angie, Lindsey knew there must be trouble. Angie did histrionics regularly, but she rarely lost control. Whatever had happened, Lindsey could tell—even from her sleep—that this was not a performance.

An hour later Lindsey was in Angie's car, driving frantically off the Cape. She had barely stopped to explain to Angie why she was taking the car, Angie couldn't have cared or understood. Lindsey was dry-eyed and purposeful as she drove, pushed by a need she couldn't understand, a need just short of terror.

Somewhere between Buzzard's Bay and Route 495, Lindsey seemed to come to. She pulled into a gas station and parked far away from the other cars. Someone watching from a distance might have thought she was carsick. Out of the car, she leaned over and her body was racked by spasms. The sobs came first, then the tears.

After a while she straightened, fished around in the car for something, and then walked toward the bank of phones on the other side of the parking lot.

"May I speak to Carol Whittier, please?"

"Who's calling?"

What was the etiquette for phone calls at convents? Would Carol even come to the phone if she knew it was Lindsey? "I'm at a payphone and it's long distance," she said breathlessly. "It's sort of an emergency."

"Just a minute, I'll see if she's here."

At least Carol hadn't left for Peru with Gina, Lindsey thought gratefully as she waited, hoping to hear Carol's voice.

"Hello?"

It was her. "Carol, it's Lindsey. I just had to talk with you," she said in a rush, feeling her control begin to slip. "I was driving to Springfield, but then I realized you might not be there, and I . . ." She didn't get any further before the rising sobs caught her.

"Lindsey, I'm so glad to hear your voice. I've been wanting to call you, but it seemed so hard to talk on the phone. What's wrong? Can you tell me what's wrong?"

Lindsey nodded, then realized that nodding was not helpful. "Danny." She gasped his name out for the first time that day. "There's been another murder. They killed Danny."

"Oh my god." Carol's response was instant and forceful. "Oh, god, Lindsey. No, no." Lindsey knew her no's weren't denial. She could hear the shock in Carol's voice, and somehow sharing her horror, hearing it reflected back in Carol's words, helped her go on.

"It was horrible. A party out on the dunes. He was shot. The police said he was dealing drugs. Who knows what else. Carol, I should have helped him, oh, god, and I just walked away from him." Lindsey started to cry now, and Carol could hear the hysteria rising in her.

"Lindsey. Can you hear me? Listen to me. Where are you?"

"Just off the Cape."

"It doesn't make any sense for you to come here. I'll come out there. We have to be there, with Danny. I want you to go back and I want you to go to Rachel's. Will you do that? And I'll be there later tonight. I'll leave here in an hour."

Lindsey heard the sense in what Carol said and felt the calm and strength in her voice. They talked for a few minutes more, until Carol was sure that Lindsey could drive. They arranged where they would meet when Carol arrived. All of the questions Lindsey had thought she would ask Carol seemed unimportant now. Are you staying with Gina? With your Community? What happened that night when you left? Did you get my letter?

She drove back slowly, stopping several times to rest. Finally she made another call, to tell Angie, Lisa, and Ellen she was coming home, to ask if there was any more news. There wasn't. The sun was out on a glorious August day, a Sunday afternoon, and all three of them were in the living room when she called. She asked Lisa, as an afterthought, to tell the restaurant she wouldn't be in that night.

Those few moments she had seen Danny last night kept playing through her memory, a projection on a screen flashing like a crazy kaleidoscope, over and over and over. Danny slouched in the shadow of that doorway. Danny's smile, was it a half-smile? Had he been sad? Or was she only imagining that now? Danny with his hands tucked in his pockets. Danny reaching out—The new memory slammed into her consciousness. *If anything comes up, call this number, will you?* And his hand pushing a piece of paper into her hand.

Lindsey stopped in her walk from the phone to the car, trying to remember what came next. She pushed her hand deep into her shorts' pocket and pulled out a crumpled piece of paper with a number written on it, a number with a Boston area code. She stared and stared at it as though it could answer her questions, then turned and walked back to the phone.

"Hello?" The voice had a Latino accent. Lindsey was not surprised.

"Jose Alfredo?" A long pause. "This is Danny's friend, Lindsey. Is that you?"

"Si."

She took a long breath. What now? Why had she called? Why had Danny given her this number? Did he trust Jose? She didn't. She should have called the police, given them the number.

Now he was getting nervous. "Hello. Lindsey? Is anything wrong? Is Danny O.K.? Why are you calling?" His urgency increased with each question.

"No," she said weakly. "He's not O.K. You've got to come out here. Please come."

A click. The dead line buzzed in her ear.

Lindsey went to the police station first when she drove into P-town. It was easier than facing Angie, Lisa, and Ellen at home. Don Slocum was at a messy desk in the center of a large room, a phone tucked between his ear and shoulder. Eddie, the dispatcher, stopped her as she came into the room. When she told him she'd seen Danny last night, he took her over to Slocum's desk.

Slocum took the crumpled piece of paper from her after he'd heard her story. She could tell by his face he was sorry she'd called, warned Jose Alfredo. "He's probably skipped," he said matter-of-factly, "but we'll send somebody to check it out as soon as we can get an address for this number."

"Danny was my friend," Lindsey heard herself saying. "Can you please tell me what happened?"

Slocum leaned back in his chair, seemed to weigh something about Lindsey's stance, attitude. She must have passed muster. His chair came forward; he leaned his arms on his desk. "It was very ugly. I haven't seen anything like this here in Provincetown. I don't understand it, I really don't understand it, but I'm going to before we're through with this thing."

He tapped his stubby fingers on the desktop, and Lindsey could see the tension hidden behind his slouch, his slow drawling attitude. "There was a party out at Head of the Meadow last night. From what we can tell, it started with high school kids drinking beer. It must have gone to heavier stuff than that because we picked up a lot of drug paraphernalia when we did our sweep this morning. They had some RVs out on the beach, even though it's a restricted area." He meant that the dune buggies weren't allowed that far up. It was an area where the park service was trying to restore the dunes. Lindsey nodded.

"We don't know what your friend was doing there, or how he got there. You say he meant to leave town. We'll check it out." He was doodling now on the pad in front of him.

"My housemate heard he was beaten up. And that you thought he was dealing drugs. That was the word Angie got in town this morning, but it isn't true. Danny couldn't have done that." Lindsey paused, afraid to know the answer to her question. "*Was* he beaten up?" Did they hurt him? she wanted to ask, but that seemed a foolish question when someone was dead.

"I can't give out details right now," Slocum started to say, but something in Lindsey's anguish seemed to catch him. "Look. This has to stay quiet. But I'll confirm what you've heard. I'd guess he was messed up—given a lesson—before he was shot. And we have picked up some of the kids who saw him at the party, who bought from him."

He paused, troubled. "Except something doesn't fit. I don't have all the pieces and I don't know where to look for them. I don't think those kids killed him," he said grimly. "I don't think they'd kill their source. And I know these kids. They're trouble, but not that kind of trouble." He was shaking his head slowly, back and forth, as though he expected the motion to jostle the pieces of this puzzle into place.

They'd gotten Danny's home address from the restaurant. Slocum had talked to the Steins. He didn't look happy about that either. "They're coming up from New York tomorrow to identify the body," he said. "If we catch up with this Jose Alfredo, maybe I'll have something else to tell them." Almost as an afterthought, he asked Lindsey, "Did his parents know he was gay?"

Lindsey nodded. "They knew he'd had a drug problem, too. But we all believed he was in recovery, clean and sober for more than a year."

She left Slocum sitting at his desk, shaking his head dismally, and decided she was ready to go home. Carol would be here in a few more hours. Thank god.

Rachel was sitting in our living room when I walked into the house. I felt like the prodigal daughter the way everybody jumped on me. Angie's eyes were red and swollen, and she started to cry again when she saw me. Rachel told me they'd been afraid I was too upset to drive safely. I guess Carol's friend Andrea had called Rachel to say Carol was on her way and they'd better check on me. I was glad to be home, to be with these women I knew. I sank down into the sofa and then started to tell them all what I'd just finished telling Don Slocum.

"There have to be witnesses who will talk," Ellen said practically, "if all those people were out there partying. They have to be able to get somebody to break, to tell what he saw."

"I don't know," Lisa argued. "If they were all on drugs, if they all took part, they can't squeal without implicating themselves."

"That's why they give immunity and plea bargaining and things like that," Ellen insisted. "They've got to catch somebody for this one. It can't go on like this or P-town will be destroyed."

"You must feel awful, Lindsey," Angie chimed in out of nowhere. "*Why* didn't you stay with him? Oh, god, it must be awful for you."

I was looking at Angie, sort of stunned. I was blaming myself, it was true. But I hadn't expected someone else to blame me.

"Wait a minute," Rachel said quickly. "Lindsey didn't do anything wrong. She couldn't see the future, Angie. She couldn't know what was going to happen. And even if she had, how do we know she wouldn't have suffered the same fate as Danny? I think we ought to leave the blaming to the police."

Angie dissolved into tears again. "I didn't mean anything. I just feel so bad for Danny."

Rachel sent Lisa and Ellen out to bring back a pizza, gave Angie three aspirin and ordered her to bed, and finally came over to sit next to me on the couch. The arm she put around my shoulder felt like mother and home. "What do you need, Lindsey?"

A place to cry, I thought, and then rejected that. I had cried all the way back on Route 6, alone in the car, and now my head was throbbing and my sinuses felt like hell. I opted for two aspirin myself and a walk in the late-afternoon sun with Rachel.

We went out Commercial Street and ducked under the chain closing off the Post Office parking lot. It was right on the water and quiet. I sat for a minute, letting the sun bake my sinuses, grateful for Rachel's company and for the silence. I wanted to ask her why things like this happen, but it seemed too juvenile a question. I was sure she had a sophisticated and meaningful answer, but I doubted it would be relevant to what I was feeling.

"I get so depressed sometimes," Rachel said finally, slowly, musing to herself. "I don't understand why things like this happen, how people can do something like this to another person."

I thought she must have been eavesdropping in my head. "In church this morning, some people had heard there'd been another murder and they looked to me to have something to say to make sense out of it, to make meaning for them. And sometimes I feel like I don't have anything to say. It's senseless. It's insane. That's what I found myself saying this morning. If we live in a society that can kill so wantonly, then we live in a sick, insane society." She was close to tears. "That's not what people come to church to hear," she said, smiling at me ruefully.

I nodded. "It makes me glad I'm an outsider," I said, remembering an early conversation with Sheila. "When I first became a lesbian, I spent a lot of time insisting I was normal. Then somebody pointed out to me what normal meant."

I felt better when we walked back to the house. Angie was sleeping, and the pizza had just arrived. We sat around the kitchen table wolfing down the pizza. Rachel went home after telling us to call if we needed her or heard anything new. We were waiting for something, I thought, but I didn't quite know what. Lisa and Ellen went out for a walk. I was waiting for Carol, but I didn't want to think too much about her because I didn't know how she would be. I'd expected more from her than she could be once. I didn't want to do that again.

I added calling Jose Alfredo to the list of things I wished I'd done differently. By nine or so that night, I was convinced Don Slocum could have solved this case instantly if I hadn't been so stupid. At some level, though, it wasn't solving the case I really cared about. I wanted to go back and do everything over for the last several weeks— at least since Danny quit Safe Harbor—and fix it so that Danny wouldn't be gone. That kind of mind game was the only way I could keep myself from imagining what might have happened last night on the beach, how Danny felt when he went out there, what it was like to be afraid, did he know they were going to shoot him, and on and on. Time traveling was easier and accomplished no more or less.

By 9:15 Carol was there. I had decided I was going to be cool, calm, and collected. Let her know I was glad to see her, but be a little distant, self-contained, so she wouldn't feel overwhelmed. She walked through the door, opened her arms, and I fell into them, sobbing. Later she said she thought it was *me* who opened my arms and *she* fell into them sobbing. Whatever. We sat on the sofa finally, still hugging, still crying, and began to talk.

I told her everything I knew about what happened to Danny, everything I suspected, everything I feared about what I should have done differently. We covered every detail several times. There was no difference between us—we felt the same way, were responding the same way, we helped one another articulate our outrage, our fear, our loss. And then it was time to talk about us. Everything we could say about

Danny had been said.

We sat silently on the couch, arms still around one another, but I thought I could feel the space growing between us.

"Your letter made me very happy and then very sad," she said.

"I'm glad you got it," I said, on the edge of sarcastic.

"I tried to answer it," she smiled at me, sadly. "I would have answered it or come back out here to talk with you this week. But I needed to have some things resolved first, know where I was."

"I would have been happy just to know what was going on with you," I said, not letting her off that easy.

"I know." Her voice was so quiet now I couldn't have heard it if she weren't resting her head on my shoulder and whispering in my ear. "I'm sorry." It was hard to stay mad and distant under the circumstances.

I waited a while. I figured she'd tell me eventually what was going on. I wasn't going to ask again.

After a bit she straightened up on the couch, pulled her arms back to her sides, and sat staring at her hands.

"I signed a trial separation agreement yesterday. For two years. It was a decision I had to make on my own, before I saw you again."

I stared at her. This was news. "Wow. That's a big step." I put my hand on top of her hands. "Tell me what you're feeling. And what this means."

"What it means is easy. I'm going to live on my own for two years and after that I can go back if I want or make the separation permanent. It's sort of like a marriage separation." She paused and took a deep breath. "How I'm feeling?" She shook her head as though to clear it. "I went on a week's retreat to come to terms with this. By myself. With my journal. It's a good thing I wasn't still there when you called," she added suddenly, "you never would have gotten me."

I felt a panic in my heart then, at the thought of not having her here when I needed her, and I knew I would forgive her for leaving, would probably agree to almost anything to have her near me like this, sharing life with me. I put my arm back around her shoulders, and she leaned into my body, relaxing.

"It feels right. I felt incredibly heavy all during the retreat. I don't know how else to describe it. Like the weight of the world was on my shoulders as I made this decision. Then I realized I was thinking I could save the world if I stayed in my Community. As soon as I got to that notion—consciously, I mean—the rest was easy. Because that was so ludicrous. I can't save the world, I can only do my work. And I'll do my work wherever I am and whoever I'm with."

She shifted and turned toward me a little, her nose and mouth nuzzling into my neck. "Right now, I want to spend some time with you. If that's what you want."

I started to bend down and kiss her mouth. How could I want anything else? And then I stopped. There was one other thing.

"What about Gina?"

Carol looked embarrassed and resigned. "She went back to Peru yesterday. Before I came back from retreat. She'd given me an ultimatum. Go back with her to Peru by a certain date, or else. It was never about Gina, actually, and it wasn't a hard choice. I don't do well with external controls, not even when they come wrapped in love and say they're for my own good."

I kissed her then, a long, peaceful kiss. It seemed as though we were going to have some time to get to know one another after all.

This is a romance, you recall, and Carol and I were struggling toward the happy ending. You know, the *dear reader, I married her* kind of conclusion. Long shots of moonlight and apple blossoms, haunting music coming from offstage. I couldn't muster the feeling, though. In romance, only the bad guys get hurt. I had really only known Danny a few weeks, and I didn't know what he'd been doing recently, whether he'd been selling drugs, or using again himself. But I did know he wasn't one of the bad guys. He was one of ours. And he got killed. He was gone. Maybe that is one of the problems with writing gay and lesbian romances. It's harder to kid ourselves that we live in a benign world, a world that wishes us well.

Ellen and Lisa came back from their walk. I introduced them to Carol and said she'd be spending the night on the sofa, which was fine. Town was very quiet, they said, nearly spooky. No one, but no one, was at Mizmoon's or hanging out in front of the movie theater. Lisa said that was where you could buy drugs in P-town, on the street, and nobody was buying tonight unless it was in a straight bar.

Ellen had stopped by the theater and said the guys were gloomy.

One fatality was bad, two was going to ruin the summer. I started to get indignant, but she said, no, they weren't talking about money and tourist trade, they were talking about their hearts, their community. It seemed like gay men would need to do something now, organize. Not just an event, but an emergency response network. Some way to track hate crimes and hate threats more efficiently and do something about them. The faggots at the theater were saying we might lose P-town as our place, our haven, unless we did some serious work right away.

Ellen and Lisa wandered off to bed, and Carol and I curled up together on the sofa again. My back might never be the same, but I wasn't about to let go of her, not yet. We necked like kids and then started talking about a future, a future together. Carol was going back to her job at Legal Aid. She was committed to that work, and they only needed her to be a lawyer—it hardly mattered to them that she wasn't a nun. "But," she said, running a finger down the bridge of my nose and over my lower lip, "there's a Legal Aid office in most cities. I don't feel committed to staying in Springfield forever. Just for this next year I've promised them."

"Hmmm," I said profoundly, torn between speech and nibbling on her finger. "I've decided to go back to Albany and finish my degree. But what I'll do with it, what job I'll be looking for, what city I might live in, that's all still up in the air." "So maybe that's something we can talk about this year. Without making any promises, I mean."

"Right. We need to just take things slow. See how it feels. I don't want us to have expectations of one another we can't meet." That was no joke. I didn't want to turn around expecting to see Carol and find her gone again. Not if I could avoid it.

"We'll just take each day as it comes," she promised. Her fingers were massaging my lower back from under my T-shirt now, moving around in mesmerizing circles, going lower and lower toward my ass.

This was interesting. I was still filled with grief about Danny, completely immersed in the loss of him, in feeling I should have done something differently, said something that would have stopped him. And at the same time I felt the energy rising in my good old sexual gyre. It was rising past my exhaustion, past my fear, past my hesitation about rushing into things with Carol. And I could tell the same thing was happening for her. I forced her mouth open with a long kiss that was no longer so gentle and felt her breath catch, then come heavier. We had waited a long time for this. Grief doesn't drive passion out, I realized, but it does give it a slightly different flavor—this passion was hot and sweet, but there was an edge of sadness in it at the same time.

I shifted my body slightly, not letting her mouth go. I wanted my hands free to wander all over her body. My hands remembered the shape of her breasts from that night—was it a hundred years ago or more?—on the pier when we'd necked like teenagers, when we'd said yes to one another. And now my hands were aching to go back, to go home.

Out of some corner of my attention, I heard a noise in the next room, the kitchen. I tried to ignore it. Surely it was Lisa or Ellen. Surely they would have the good sense to stay out of the living room. But the noise continued and finally registered in my brain. Someone was knocking on the kitchen door.

I pulled away from Carol, explaining what was happening. I went to the door. The knock came again, quiet, persistent.

All of a sudden I was afraid. "Who is it?"

"Jose," a voice whispered, "Jose Alfredo." He had come back.

Chapter Thirteen

A fine mist filled the air the next morning when four of us left our house, packed into Angie's car for the two-block drive we would usually have walked. Rachel was waiting for us at the police station. Angie waved a good luck sign at me, Jose Alfredo, and Carol, then she went home to wait for the news. Miracles never cease, I thought, when she offered to be chauffeur with no strings attached. Rachel shook Jose Alfredo's hand, gave me and Carol a hug, then we all went in.

We hadn't needed to tell Jose that Danny was dead. He seemed to know it as soon as he came in the door and looked at me. His eyes went very sad and resigned, like he'd known it was going to happen all along. I imagined Danny trying to convince him it would be fine, and Jose going along with it, because what else was he going to do? Danny was pretty convincing when he wanted to be.

Carol had spent most of the night with Jose, going over his story. I believed it as he told it, and it made me proud to know Danny. To have known him, I mean. Even now I have trouble believing he isn't here, sharp-eyed and ready to take me on about anything.

Danny had agreed to take a last drug shipment for Jose if Jose would go to Boston and start at a drug treatment center. Danny called, got the place for him, the whole bit. And Jose went. Left on the early evening bus, before Danny was to meet the drugs coming in. Danny had called late that night, accusing Jose of a betrayal. The drug runner had no intentions of letting a good connection go.

"You told me this was the last shipment, Jose. You said they'd let you go after this one."

"That's what they told me, amigo." We could hear the anguish in his voice as he sat in our kitchen at two o'clock in the morning remembering this conversation.

"Danny, I'm here, waiting for you to call. I wouldn't be here if I betrayed you," Jose pleaded. "What happened, man, tell me what happened?"

"They treated me like an idiot. Like they couldn't imagine I would think this was it." Danny would have hated that, I knew, sitting there, watching Jose closely as he told this story. "I had to take the stuff to a drop, and I've got a bag full of money that has to go somewhere else tomorrow, and this guy knows me now."

Jose and Danny had learned that night what being known meant, and Jose explained it to Carol. She had offered to represent him when we went into the P.D. "They have their ways. Once they I.D. you, you're theirs. You can't work for another dealer, that's death. You can't not show up with the stuff or the money. No matter where you go, you'll be dead."

So Danny was trapped, or felt he was. And if he was caught in this muck, he decided he was going to take the whole P-town drug trade with him. It was the only way he could see out.

"Was he using again, Jose?" I had to ask, I wanted to know, but I held my breath against the answer.

"No, man. He was crazy against the stuff. He was hanging out with those guys, but he was trying to get evidence. That's what he told me. He was trying to figure out their network. He said he'd be back in Boston in a couple of days, and we'd take it to the cops."

"What evidence, Jose? Did he send you stuff?"

"No, man. I was doing the rehab thing during the day, staying at Danny's apartment."

"Day treatment?" I asked, surprised. But of course. That was why he'd answered the phone when I called.

"That was all he could get me. He said he didn't want me to think about anything except what they were telling me at the rehab about getting off the stuff." But they had talked, of course. We sat on the edge of our chairs as Jose told us how Danny had started hearing some of the dealers talk about the murder out on the dunes. How one of the local sellers thought the kid was a connection for a big drug drop on the beach. The kid was in a gay bar, thought they were picking him up for sex. Jose didn't know too many details. He said Danny had been shocked at how some of the locals hated the gays who came out to P-town. Mostly the dealers Danny was hanging out with at Murphy's bar treated that murder like a joke. Danny wasn't sure if the dead man had been dealing or not, but he was gay and some-body had wanted to make an example of him.

"Did he find out who he was? Where he was from?"

"Not really. Probably he'd been living in Boston and came out here because he'd heard it was O.K. for gay people. Danny thought he was Cuban, maybe, but nobody knew for sure."

I thought about that for a minute and how we had joked about anonymity on the beach the next day. It didn't seem so funny now—maybe it hadn't really been funny then either, just a way of letting go of the tension we were all feeling. That young man had dropped like a shell on the beach, come from nowhere, attached to no one. It frightened me.

"Why did Danny want me to call you," I wondered suddenly, "if you didn't have any evidence?"

"I was his friend." Jose was quiet and dignified in his protest.

"I know," I apologized. "Do you think he had all the evidence on him when he was killed? Is that why they killed him?"

Jose shrugged. He didn't know. And Carol's eyes were starting to cross with fatigue. We took a break then. Locked the kitchen door for the first time the whole summer. Gave Jose the couch. And Carol and I curled up on my narrow bed for a couple of hours of chaste repose before sunrise.

When we walked into the P.D. at nine in the morning, it didn't look any more busy than it had on a Sunday afternoon, and it was pos-sible Slocum hadn't moved since then. He was in the same pose, phone under his chin.

He looked eager when I introduced Jose Alfredo Mendez to him. I saw an almost greedy smile cross his face, then flicker out when we introduced Carol as Jose's attorney. Rachel and I had to leave them then, but Rachel made a point of telling Carol she was available for whatever was needed. She meant bond or bail money, but as we

walked toward the Sunshine Cafe, she said she'd wanted Don Slocum to know he was being watched by someone who lived right here
in town.

"Things have a way of happening too conveniently, sometimes,"
she said. "Don can't find a witness he'd had the week before, so
charges against somebody he went to high school with are dropped.
That sort of thing. It happens in every small town, I guess. But out
here it has a way of happening when gay people bring the complaints
or are the victims. We haven't gotten a whole lot of satisfaction out
of Don."

I inhaled my first mug of coffee and was starting to sip the second
when my brain clicked in with the constant stream of questions I
usually live with. I'd been so tired and confused, I hadn't even missed
them.

"I don't get it," I said to myself and Rachel. "Jose isn't the key to
this. He doesn't know who killed Danny and Danny didn't give him
evidence. Why did Danny want me to call him? What did that mes-
sage mean, then?"

Rachel gave me that sweet smile people sometimes have when they
are about to explain the obvious.

"I expect Danny felt threatened, Lindsey. And he loved Jose Alfredo
and didn't want him to be sitting, wondering what happened. And
maybe he thought you'd be able to give Jose some help. If they were
lovers, this is going to be rough for him, really rough."

Oh. Of course. Not what Jose Alfredo could do for me, but what
I could do for him. Danny was still taking care of. Rachel was right.
It made sense.

"Then we don't have any idea who killed Danny or how to find
that out," I realized. That was depressing. We both sat pondering it
for a moment.

"I'm afraid it sounds like that may be true," Rachel agreed reluc-
tantly.

I walked alone back to the house. The landscape around me had
changed drastically in the last twenty-four hours. Yesterday it had
been a town bustling with tourists enjoying themselves, laughing,
window-shopping, threatened by an occasional drunk puking on the
sidewalk, nothing more. It had been a place where dykes like me could

walk safely alone or hand in hand with a lover. Where faggots like Danny could play out their dreams—rescuing knight or intriguing stranger—the end of the game should never have been death.

Carol came home alone, looking grim.

"I think we need some help," she said, sagging into the sofa. "I wish we were doing this in Springfield, or even Boston. I think I need to get the Feds here, soon."

"Where is he? Did you need bail?"

Carol was shaking her head, no. "I think he's safer in jail, but, Lindsey, I'm afraid for him. Something about this just isn't right."

She told me a little more of Jose's story. He came into this country illegally to sell drugs. That made his situation now real tenuous. Coming forward had cost him a lot, in one sense. Maybe Danny had known that and wanted to warn him to flee. But he hadn't. He came out here to see if Danny needed him. Jose could identify quite a few of the dealers operating in P-town, but that wasn't much use unless a cop wanted to work to develop evidence, set the dealer up for sales to cops, that sort of thing. The Feds would do it in a minute, but Slocum wasn't interested.

I told Carol what Rachel had said about witnesses disappearing when it suited Slocum. She nodded, thinking. "It may be. He may know more about the drug trade than he wants to. Usually in a place like this it's outsiders who come in with the stuff and involve local people in the selling."

"Remember what he said when he wanted us to call off the march?" It was vague, but I knew it had irritated me when I heard it. "Something about 'not bothering the tourists.' He didn't sound real interested in law enforcement, just making it safe for people to spend their money. Maybe he doesn't care what happens to the people who spend their money on drugs. He figures he's only here for the people who are selling the stuff." I paused. "God, do you think he could be one of the sellers?"

She got up abruptly, reenergized. "I need to make some phone calls."

In an hour she was done. She looked utterly drained. I took her in my arms and held her for a long moment without asking a single question. That seemed to perk her up a bit.

"I think I just called in every favor anyone might have owed me in the past or might possibly owe me in the next ten years," she said finally. "I sure hope I'm right about this."

"What happens now?" I wanted to know.

"We wait. He's as safe as he can be in jail. I expect some Feds will be getting in touch with Mr. Slocum very soon. And I have a room waiting for me at Maggie's guesthouse."

I hadn't let her out of my arms yet and wasn't in a hurry to do so. "I expect you'll need some help, getting your heavy suitcase out of the car, carrying it up those steep stairs and all." Suddenly I remembered. "You don't have any roommates, do you?"

She was laughing at me, I was glad to see. "No roommates. And yes, my deodorant and toothbrush weigh a ton and I was counting on you to help me get them up the stairs."

The stairs were too narrow to climb them side by side. Carol went ahead with the key to her room, and I followed with her daypack slung over my shoulder. It was not a heavy burden, but my heart beat loudly.

Some events are symbolic even before they happen. You wait and wait for them and they get weighted down with meaning. Occasionally the event is far less important than all the anticipation, all the preparation. I worried about that while Carol turned the key in the door, stepped into the room, and then moved aside for me to come in too. It was a little room under the eaves, with a big double bed taking up most of the floor space. That was just fine with me. I stopped worrying about symbolism.

She locked the door from the inside and stood for a moment, her head leaning against the closed door. I waited quietly for her to turn around. It wasn't like when Beryl Chatham read about the lovers being reunited after three years and everything was green and flowing. We weren't even lovers yet, but what we had been through together was affecting this moment. And what we'd been through alone. I knew Carol was thinking about Springfield, maybe about Gina, but certainly about her Community and what it meant that today she was starting her life without them, her new life on her own. I was remembering the night at the memorial service when Carol and I had lit our candles and then I'd turned around to see her disappearing. And I was remembering Belle and the life we were planning together, when one day I turned around and she was gone. Was I ready to take this chance?

And then it didn't much matter if my head decided it was ready or not, because Carol turned around and stepped toward me and took both of my hands in hers, and I realized my heart was already there. I might as well follow.

"When I said I was used to delayed gratification," Carol said softly, "I never thought it would be more than a few hours, a couple of days at most. I'm so glad you're still here, Lindsey."

Our eyes were just about level with one another. Green, her eyes were green. I remembered my shock and joy at first seeing them look directly at me like this, and once again—I swear—I could see moon-light on still ocean water and hear the sound of the lonesome fog-horn moaning offshore.

"I'm a little scared," she said.

"Me, too," I agreed, and leaned forward to kiss her lips, a light brush, a foreshadowing. "We shouldn't rush into making promises and as-sumptions, I guess."

"That's right." She was unbuttoning my blue workshirt, starting at the top, letting her fingers barely touch my quickly heating skin. "We should just take things as they come. No long-term commit-ments." I could feel her breath on my left earlobe.

"Right." I shuddered as she slid my shirt off my shoulders. She stepped back to look at me, and I waited a minute. "This is about sex, we should realize, not commitment." I stopped her hand as she moved her fingers toward my shorts. It was my turn. I slid both hands under her blouse and pulled it off over her head without waiting to unbutton it.

"Mmmm." Her nipples were already hard. My voice was deceptively casual, more like Ra's than mine. I wanted her now. I didn't want to wait, could hardly imagine any more foreplay. Desire overwhelmed me, rose like a tidal wave, and pushed me forward.

"Carol," and this time it was urgent. "I can't wait. I want you now. Now."

"Oh, thank god," she muttered in my neck as we fell back onto the bed. I felt her mouth fasten on mine and her tongue probe deep into my mouth. It was the permission we had both been waiting for.

She only moved away for a minute to pull my shorts off, then her own. And then her fingers were on me, in me, finding hidden places that were waiting to be found, to be opened by her. I barely knew this woman, and my body had been waiting for her all of my life.

With Ra I had explored my fears, explored the darker side of my lust, and found it not so fearful after all. I let my body remember those lessons as Carol and I led one another into the peaks and valleys of passion. I could lose myself in what I was feeling and not fear I would lose her, I could take from her what I wanted and know that she was receiving while I took. I knew now how to keep my tongue right on the hard button of her clitoris, even while my hands played with her nipples, even while her body thrashed, heaved with desire underneath me. This first loving was not gentle between us. We had waited too long. I was half afraid of hurting her, but when my nails dug into her back, my mouth clamped on her breast, I heard her breathe, "Yes yes, harder, harder," and I let myself go wherever my body took me, let myself push her hard over that edge where passion becomes satisfaction.

We must have slept, exhausted, satisfied, but in no way satiated. As I dozed off, her fingers still deep in my cunt, I knew there would be more. I trusted that for the first time as I lay fighting sleep, wanting to go on hearing her deep-sleep breath next to my ear forever.

I was jerked out of a dream—I think it was a cottage with a white picket fence, goddess help me—by someone pounding, pounding on the door, calling our names. "Carol, Lindsey. Hello. Is anyone in there? A phone call for one of you, and she says it's an emergency. Hello? Hello? Can I tell her you're coming?"

"Yes," Carol mumbled to the door, looking around like she couldn't remember her name or me or where she was. Dark had come while we slept, and it could have been a different planet, I had been so far away.

She put on her shorts and my shirt and went down the hall. When she came back moving fast, I was glad I had spent my few moments unbuttoning her blouse and turning it right side out.

"Rachel," she said cryptically. "We have to go to the Police Department. Now."

We left the car and went racing down the two blocks. Eddy had called Rachel, Carol told me breathlessly. Slocum wanted to release Jose before the Feds came. Said he didn't have anything to hold him for. As though being illegally in the country wasn't anything. Eddy was worried. Rachel was worried. From the way we were running, I could tell we were worried, too, but I didn't quite know why.

But I did two seconds later when we came screeching around the corner, and there—parked right in front of the P.D. like it was town equipment or something—was the black truck I'd been tripping over all month. Parked as though it was waiting for something. Or someone. Somebody was in it, somebody I couldn't see, and the engine was idling softly, just like that night in the alley. Danny had been in that truck, I realized suddenly, and he'd lied to me about it.

We walked into Slocum's office, right past Eddy, over to where Rachel was standing at his desk, waving her arms and talking fervently.

"Where is Jose Alfredo?" Carol interrupted her.

Slocum looked up at her. He was more animated than I'd ever seen him, but in him that was not an attractive state. He was mad, is what I mean, and he wasn't trying to be polite.

"I'm trying to get the fucking paperwork done here so I can have Eddy bring him up and we can get him out of here." I raised an eyebrow. Swearing in front of someone he'd called Rev. Smythe the month before? Tch. Tch. We must have interrupted something.

I didn't know what they wanted, to get Jose out or keep him in, so I left them to it and wandered over to Eddy's station by the door. He gave me a wan smile. His phone call had served us well, but if Slocum suspected why we were here, Eddy's life would be hell.

"Eddy," I asked on an impulse, "who owns that black truck out front. You know, the one with all the chrome and the bank of lights across the top."

He didn't look happy I'd asked. "Uhh, there are a couple like that around." He shrugged, trying to dismiss it.

"This one is sitting out front now with the engine running, sort of double-parked. Is that the Chief's truck?" I prodded him with the improbable.

"Nah. But it might be his brother-in-law's." Now he was being a little more helpful. "Frank. Francesco Salazar. Owns one of the smaller lobster fleets that operates out of the harbor. Could be him. He's got a couple of trucks for the business, I think."

I was beginning to figure out what that meant when the door opened and two gentlemen who couldn't have been anything but Feds presented themselves to Eddy. Goddess, I thought, could they have tried harder to dress for the part? Beige trench coats, ties pulled slightly loose, top shirt-collar buttons undone, hair not quite short enough to be a crew cut, but definitely government issue. The one in front pulled his wallet out of his right hip pocket, just like in the movies, and waved it at Eddy, who pointed toward Slocum. I saw Carol step back from his desk as they approached, relief all over her face.

She explained it to us later over dinner at Rachel's. "Slocum got a call that the Feds were on the way. Lucky for us he didn't get too much notice. They called to make sure he held on to Jose for them, but his first response was to get the guy out. When Rachel got there, Slocum was about ready to turn him loose on the street."

"Why would that matter?" I wanted to know. "Jose wasn't going to run anywhere. He wanted to tell his story. He would have waited for the Feds, no?"

"I'm afraid that if Jose had walked out of the P.D. without an escort, he would have disappeared." She interrupted my protest. "Not willingly. But for good. These guys have killed twice. I'm sure it was the same person—or people—in both murders. And I don't think there would have even been a body to find this time."

Oh. All of a sudden it jolted me. I told them what Eddy had said about the truck and who owned it. And what I'd seen the night of the march when Danny got out of it.

"Wow. I'll bet Jose knows something about that. I'll call Brian in the morning and let him know where to start." Brian was one of the Feds in Boston who'd responded to Carol's urgent request.

Rachel fed us and patted us both on the head—metaphorically speaking, I mean—for doing good work. And then it was time, past time, to go home.

We stood together in the dark outside Rachel's door. Now what? I wondered. We said no commitment. Should I offer to go home and let her have some space?

"You can borrow my toothbrush," was all she had to say.

I took her hand, and we walked out toward the lights of Commercial Street. Tonight, in the dark, the ominous, perilous street I had walked down earlier seemed to have gone back to being itself. Tourists were only tourists. The stores were closing, and the bars and clubs were starting to get noisier. The air was warm tonight, a summer night in August, and I was walking down the street, hand in hand with the woman I loved.

Chapter Fourteen

Should I end here? The rest, as they say, is history. You may have read about the huge drug sweeps on the outer Cape at the end of August. They picked up half a million dollars worth of cocaine, plenty of cash, lots of low-level dealers, and a couple of the big guys. One Francesco Salazar was named in the indictments, but the sweep missed him. Wherever he went, a warrant is waiting for him back in P-town.

Some of the kids arrested for dealing had been out at the beach the night Salazar brought Danny out and dropped him in the middle of their party. They'd roughed him up some, but swore he was alive when Frank took him off into the dunes. The Feds added murder to the indictment. The first murder in the dunes was never solved, but Jose and I are pretty sure Salazar was involved in that one, too. He'd thought someone else was trying to muscle in on his turf, Jose said, and got nervous. A gay dealer with gay connections could do very well in P-town.

I privately thought it had more to do with someone hating gay people, being afraid of us in some deep place that turned fear to hatred. I couldn't imagine mutilating a human being that way for profit. There was hatred in that murder, it wasn't only a drug turf war. And although I hadn't seen a lot the night I'd stopped into Murphy's Bar and Grill, I knew the men there would have hated Danny for being gay. Was that why they killed him? Or was it part of it? I couldn't begin to guess. Life just isn't that neat. It's like asking questions about love. Why did Danny love Jose Alfredo? Why did I love Carol? And what does any of it mean anyway?

Jose is in a witness protection program. I saw him in September just before school started. He was really proud of his three months clean and sober. After the trials, he'll be given a green card that will make him a legal immigrant under a new name. He's looking forward to starting life over again. We talked about Danny a little, and we cried together. Jose isn't gay and Danny knew that, at the end. But they loved one another—we were brothers, Jose insisted—and I like to think that would make Danny very happy.

The Steins buried Danny traditionally, in a Jewish cemetery in New York, but late in August his mother called Rachel and said some of his AA friends wanted a memorial service in Boston in the fall. Would Rachel let his friends in Provincetown know?

I went alone. Carol was back in Springfield, working on a case she couldn't leave. I held my lit candle and had a long talk with Danny about love and the choices we make for love, the risks we take for love. I learned a lot from you, Daniel Stein, I told him. I looked around at the full room, at the dozens of candles flickering in the hands of women and men who had loved Danny.

Gradually, one by one, people stood up and said something about Danny. Funny stories. Things he had done that helped, things he had done that were hard. This was definitely the Danny I had known. I recognized him in every tale. With each story, Danny was more and more present in the room.

"Danny loved the idea of community," said a short heavy-set woman I'd seen occasionally out at the Cape, "but community didn't come easy to him." A few people nodded in agreement, and I wondered what she meant. "If he had been able to include us in his last difficulty, he might still be with us. But Danny tried to solve the problem himself. He never picked up the phone. He forgot you don't recover in isolation. You can't do it alone." She sat down, and I sensed a change in the room. The grief was still sharp, but there was something else there, too.

"Marjorie is right," said the next man who stood up. He was older, white-haired, and portly, and he certainly didn't look gay to me. "Danny didn't die because he wanted to help, to reach out to a fellow addict. I think it's important for us to remember that. We all want to help. We do it every day, first by being sober ourselves. It's not a criticism of Danny to say he made a mistake. We all make mistakes. Recovery doesn't make us perfect, just better than when we were drunk." He paused for the laugh, and I thought he'd probably used that line before. "It's just that usually in sobriety we get a chance to make amends for our mistakes. I wish he'd reached out, just made that one phone call. I want to remember Danny the next time I think I can do it better by myself. I think that's how I'll be able to keep him with me, keep that wonderful crazy guy close to me." He was weeping as he sat down and didn't seem to mind who saw.

That was the turn it took for the next few speakers before the hour was over—how can we take something from what happened and give it meaning in our lives? And so Danny's senseless death began to connect us, make community out of all these different people. I thought I could see Danny, head tilted to one side, sort of nodding in agreement.

The rest of August in P-town was fairly quiet for our house. I spent some nights with Carol, who stayed a couple of weeks. I was back working at Safe Harbor, and she would come in late and we'd walk home together. We needed the quiet to learn to know one another. I liked the woman I was meeting.

Knowing Carol quieted some of my fears about what I had been learning from Ra. Exploring different parts of me wasn't so bad, and Ra was right: if I hadn't discovered them, I couldn't decide if I liked them or wanted to use them or change them. Ra, Joan, and Gabrielle met Carol one night at the restaurant. We all hung out at Mizmoon's for a while later that night, and walking home I told Carol a little about Ra and me. Not all of it, mind you. That wasn't necessary. She pondered the essentials and didn't say much at first. But when we were in bed, hugging and stroking one another, she asked, "Should I worry about losing you to Ra?"

"I don't think Ra wants me," I joked. Then I was serious. "No," I said. "I want to learn myself with you right now." She understood what I meant.

Oh, yes, there was one exception to the quiet. We were sitting in the living room with popcorn and TV one night when Angie came in. Behind her was Rico, her Portuguese friend who ran the bakery two stores over from Angie's import business. He looked nervous, very nervous.

Angie took his hand and drew him forward. "I want to say something to all of you," she said. "I've been seeing Rico." She stopped. I just stared. It seemed like all of us were speechless. What *was* she talking about?

"Oh, my god," Ellen broke the silence, turned accusingly to Lisa. "This is what you were hiding from me. Oh my god, Angie, you can't be serious. He's a MAN." As though that fact might have escaped Angie.

"I want you to know," Angie continued, "that I still consider myself a lesbian. I don't feel any different inside. It's just that I happen to be loving Rico for now," she smiled up at him lovingly, in case we missed it.

"And I don't want to have to hide from my own friends. I want to be able to have a lover come here, too. Just like Lindsey does," she finished on a note of defiance.

Well, I had to give her credit. She had courage. I wouldn't have liked to walk into that room with a lover who had a penis and have to face the four of us. Lisa, Ellen, me, Carol. We argued with her for a while, but she'd practiced her lines and it was a bit like the night when we discussed Morningstar Moondaughter's past lives. Impasse. Except this time Lisa wasn't quite so involved. In fact, she looked a little pensive.

After Angie and Rico left I asked her what she was thinking, had she known this before? She'd guessed it. Figured it was Angie's business. She'd been Angie's friend all these years because, basically, Angie had a good heart. So she'd trust Angie's heart this time, too, she figured. Lisa never was one who wanted to argue theory or abstractions. She liked dealing with what was right in front of her.

"Not me," I told Carol, as we walked back to her room. "I *know* what it means to be a lesbian, and it doesn't mean having a lover with a penis."

"Maybe Angie means being a lesbian is a state of mind," Carol suggested. "You know, it's about how you see the world."

"But you see the world differently if your lover is of the opposite sex, because that's *legal*," I insisted. I knew this, at least. I could be sure of this. I thought.

"What about a woman who has never had a lover? Couldn't she be a lesbian? Is being a lesbian a permanent thing? Like being a certain race or having a certain color hair? Face it, Lindsey. We really don't know a whole lot about what it means to be a lesbian."

I was learning real quick that arguing with a lawyer can take a lot of time and preparation. I let it drop for then because we were climbing those narrow steps again, Carol ahead, me behind. I put both hands under her ass as she climbed. "I don't know about legal definitions," I told her, "but I'd be glad to show you in person what I think a lesbian is."

And I did.

Other titles from Firebrand Books include:

Beneath My Heart, Poetry by Janice Gould/$8.95

The Big Mama Stories by Shay Youngblood/$8.95

A Burst Of Light, Essays by Audre Lorde/$7.95

Crime Against Nature, Poetry by Minnie Bruce Pratt/$8.95

Diamonds Are A Dyke's Best Friend by Yvonne Zipter/$9.95

Dykes To Watch Out For, Cartoons by Alison Bechdel/$6.95

Exile In The Promised Land, A Memoir by Marcia Freedman/$8.95

Eye Of A Hurricane, Stories by Ruthann Robson / $8.95

The Fires Of Bride, A Novel by Ellen Galford/$8.95

A Gathering Of Spirit, A Collection by North American Indian Women edited by Beth Brant *(Degonwadonti)*/$9.95

Getting Home Alive by Aurora Levins Morales and Rosario Morales/$8.95

Good Enough To Eat, A Novel by Lesléa Newman/$8.95

Humid Pitch, Narrative Poetry by Cheryl Clarke/$8.95

Jewish Women's Call For Peace edited by Rita Falbel, Irena Klepfisz, and Donna Nevel/$4.95

Jonestown & Other Madness, Poetry by Pat Parker/$7.95

The Land Of Look Behind, Prose and Poetry by Michelle Cliff/$6.95

A Letter To Harvey Milk, Short Stories by Lesléa Newman/$8.95

Letting In The Night, A Novel by Joan Lindau/$8.95

Living As A Lesbian, Poetry by Cheryl Clarke/$7.95

Making It, A Woman's Guide to Sex in the Age of AIDS by Cindy Patton and Janis Kelly/$4.95

Metamorphosis, Reflections On Recovery, by Judith McDaniel/$7.95

Mohawk Trail by Beth Brant *(Degonwadonti)*/$7.95

Moll Cutpurse, A Novel by Ellen Galford/$7.95

More Dykes To Watch Out For, Cartoons by Alison Bechdel/$7.95

The Monarchs Are Flying, A Novel by Marion Foster/$8.95

Movement In Black, Poetry by Pat Parker/$8.95

My Mama's Dead Squirrel, Lesbian Essays on Southern Culture by Mab Segrest/$8.95

New, Improved! Dykes To Watch Out For, Cartoons by Alison Bechdel/$7.95

The Other Sappho, A Novel by Ellen Frye/$8.95

Politics Of The Heart, A Lesbian Parenting Anthology edited by Sandra Pollack and Jeanne Vaughn/$11.95

Presenting. . . Sister NoBlues by Hattie Gossett/$8.95

A Restricted Country by Joan Nestle/$8.95

Sacred Space by Geraldine Hatch Hanon/$9.95

Sanctuary, A Journey by Judith McDaniel/$7.95

Sans Souci, And Other Stories by Dionne Brand/$8.95

Scuttlebutt, A Novel by Jana Williams/$8.95

Shoulders, A Novel by Georgia Cotrell/$8.95

Simple Songs, Stories by Vickie Sears/$8.95

The Sun Is Not Merciful, Short Stories by Anna Lee Walters/$7.95

Tender Warriors, A Novel by Rachel Guido deVries/$8.95

This Is About Incest by Margaret Randall/$7.95

The Threshing Floor, Short Stories by Barbara Burford/$7.95

Trash, Stories by Dorothy Allison/$8.95

The Women Who Hate Me, Poetry by Dorothy Allison/$8.95

Words To The Wise, A Writer's Guide to Feminist and Lesbian Periodicals & Publishers by Andrea Fleck Clardy/$4.95

Yours In Struggle, Three Feminist Perspectives on Anti-Semitism and Racism by Elly Bulkin, Minnie Bruce Pratt, and Barbara Smith/$8.95

You can buy Firebrand titles at your bookstore, or order them directly from the publisher (141 The Commons, Ithaca, New York 14850, 607-272-0000).

Please include $2.00 shipping for the first book and $.50 for each additional book.

A free catalog is available on request.